I recognized the symbols right away—it was Lorielle, and she had sent us a message! I dashed over to my backpack and pulled out my angel language decoder.

"What is it?" Annie asked. "What's going on?"

"I'll tell you in a minute!" I said. I wrote furiously, decoding Lori's message. When I finally translated it, my mouth dropped open in shock.

"Tell me!" Annie practically screamed.

"Your brother…," I said. I frowned and read it again, just to make sure.

"What?" cried Annie. *"What?"*

"It's your brother…Zack," I said. "He's been kidnapped!"

Hannah and the Angels

Notes from Blue Mountain

by Linda Lowery Keep

Based on a concept by
Linda Lowery Keep
and Carole Newhouse

Random House 🏠 New York

www.randomhouse.com/kids

Library of Congress Cataloging-in-Publication Data
Keep, Linda Lowery.
Hannah and the angels: notes from blue mountain /
by Linda Lowery Keep.
SUMMARY: Continues the adventures of eleven-year-old Hannah, who
finds herself mysteriously transported to the Appalachian Mountains,
where the angels have sent her to accomplish a special mission.
ISBN: 0-679-89161-7
[1. Angels—Fiction. 2. Space and time—Fiction. 3. Adventures and adven-
turers—Fiction. 4. Appalachian Mountains—Fiction] I. Title.
II. Series: Keep, Linda Lowery. Hannah and the angels: bk. #4

Printed in the United States of America
10 9 8 7 6 5 4 3 2

For Mother Nature's angels,
who've kept watch over the mountains
for millions of years.
May they help us keep them green and lively.

" See that you do not look down
on one of these little ones. For I
tell you that their angels in
heaven always see the face of
my Father in heaven."

Matthew 18:10

Nancy Ls Samacki
Dec. 2012

Acknowledgments

I gratefully acknowledge the people from West Virginia who helped make Hannah's trip to Appalachia a wonderful writing adventure for me:

Mary Cleminson, of Shepherdstown, whose work has provided computers and computer education to so many children like Annie, and who started my trek up those imaginary hollers.

Mary Lucille DeBerry, a WNPB producer in Morgantown, who set me straight on ramps, ghost stories, horseradish pickles, and so many of the cultural treasures of the Appalachian region.

Myra Bonhage-Hale, an herbalist from Alum Bridge, who told me about pink sumac lemonade, the poisonous jack-o'-lantern, and the angels who live in the mountains.

And last, but far from least, I thank Kenneth LaFreniere of Random House, who edited my story with humor and sincerity.

Contents

Hannah and the Angels

Notes from Blue Mountain

Chapter 1

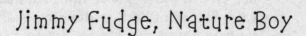

Jimmy Fudge, Nature Boy

Some boys can be so stupid. Especially boys named Jimmy Fudge.

There we were on a nature trip with our teacher, Ms. Crybaby, just outside of Geneva, Wisconsin, where we live. (Her real name is Ms. Crysler.) We were making notes and drawing the plants we saw in our science notebooks.

"This is sumac," said Ms. Crybaby, pointing. She pronounced it SOO-mack.

The fields and woods were fiery red regular sumac from all the sumac bushes. They were really beautiful.

"There are two varieties of sumac," she reminded us for the hundredth time. "Regular and poison."

So guess which kind Jimmy Fudge decided to pick up and rub all over his face? Right! The poison kind, of course.

poison sumac

1

"You're a cheesehead, Fudge!" yelled Kevin McPherson.

"That's enough, boys!" said Ms. Crybaby.

Fudge

But Jimmy Fudge kept right on rubbing the poison leaf on his face. "Hey, Martin, look!" he said, grinning at me.

My friend Katie nudged me with her elbow. "Just ignore him, Hannah," she said. She went back to drawing acorns.

"So, Hannah, how come I never got to go on angel trips with you?" she said casually.

I wasn't sure what to say. Katie and her twin brother, David, are my best friends. But the missions I get sent on to help other kids in different places of the world are up to my angels. (I'll tell you more about them later.) I don't have any control over where they send me. I never know when they're going to drop me in the middle of somewhere. And as far as I know, they only send me, Hannah, all by myself. I have no idea why. Maybe I could ask the angels about letting me take a friend with me next time. If there *is* a next time. So far, I'd been to Australia, Kenya, and Mexico. But maybe that's the end of it.

Katie's acorns

"Do you mean you feel left out?" I asked Katie as I drew a cattail bursting open. All the soft, fuzzy cotton that holds the seeds was fluffing out. *Like little bunny tails*, I wrote next to my picture.

"Yeah, sure I do," said Katie, making a fake pouty face. "If I can't go with you, you could at *least* keep a journal of your trips so your best friend in the whole world can read about them. Don't you think?"

like little bunny tails ↓

my cattail drawing

"Sounds like a good idea." I agreed. "Next time I go, I promise I'll keep notes for you." Actually, I was already keeping a journal of my missions. I just hadn't been ready to share it with anyone yet, I guess.

"Cool," said Katie. "Just like the notes and pictures we're doing now?"

"Okay," I said.

"So where *are* you going next?" Katie asked.

"I have no idea." I said truthfully. "One minute, I'm on a field trip with you. The next minute, I could be in Timbuktu riding a yak."

"Girls, let's get back to the project over there," Ms. Crysler called.

I continued with my cattail and Katie colored in her acorns. Jimmy Fudge, however, kept rubbing the sumac leaves all over his face. And the more attention he got from everyone, the more he rubbed. He was acting all macho, like the poison would never bother him. I couldn't wait to see his face blow up like a balloon (which actually might be an improvement from what's already attached to his neck).

Ms. Crybaby just stood there with her arms crossed, waiting. I think she's finally realized that the only way to handle Jimmy is to ignore him. If she had tried to stop him, he probably would have behaved even worse. So she just pretended as if he weren't even there.

Ms. Crybaby

Just as the Fudge's face was about to swell up like an ugly bloated pumpkin, I began to hear music traveling through the trees. It sounded like a violin that was being played really fast.

As I listened, my stomach began to feel a little jumpy. The music got louder and louder. Then, as soft, dreamy sounds mixed in with the peppy melody, I knew it was Lyra, my musical angel. Only she could make music so amazing.

And just like that, I was gone. Too bad, because I was about to see Jimmy Fudge's head explode. But little did I know I was about to meet a boy even more irritating than the Fudgemaster himself.

Chapter 2

Quilts and Fiddles and Firelight Tales

Suddenly, I was sitting on a tree stump. My notebook was open to the cattail drawing. I still had my red knapsack. But Katie was gone. Ms. Crybaby was gone. The class was gone. And there was no fiery Fudge face in sight. I could still hear that violin music. Violins sound sad sometimes, like they're crying. But this one sounded really happy. I flipped to a new page, in my notebook and quickly wrote:

Wednesday afternoon

Dear Katie,

Guess what? I'm here already—on another angel trip!

I'm not in Timbuktu (I don't think) but...hmmm...let's see.

Here's what's around me:

    1. Fast, happy violin music.

    2. Lots of mountains. Big ones.

3. Trees, trees, trees—red and orange and yellow.
4. Little log cabins tucked here and there in the trees. (I'm sitting outside one of them.)
5. Lots of people hanging around in the yard, playing music, dancing, eating.

Maybe I'm at a family reunion. I'll check it out.
Later, Hannah.

Where am I ?

I shut my journal, got up from the stump, and headed toward the log house.

"Welcome," said a big, friendly-sounding man. He was dressed like my dad. (He always wears jeans and plaid shirts.) "You must be Jake Smith's girl."

"Uh, no," I said. "I'm Hannah. Hannah Martin."

"Oh! One of the Martin girls! You sure have grown some!" he said. He grinned as if he was super-proud of me.

I didn't say anything. Sometimes it's better for me just to keep my mouth shut.

"Well, Hannah, you can call me John. Now come on in! You look a little hungry." He opened the screen door to the cabin for me, and I walked inside. John introduced me to everyone there like I was a long-lost relative. They all said how glad they were to see me. But the strange thing was, they didn't even know me!

So, where had my angels sent me now? Everybody spoke American-sounding English, which meant I was in the United States or maybe Canada. There were also a lot of trees and mountains in this place. I started going through my brain files from Ms. Crybaby's geography class. Where were the North American mountain chains? I figured that I had to be in the Rockies, the Ozarks, the Appalachians, or the Laurentians. But which one?

"Glad you came, Hannah." A boy with a violin in his hand nodded to me. "My dad's our people-greeter today. I'm Zack." Zack had red hair and twinkly brown eyes. His jeans had a purple bandanna tied below one knee. "So, which group are you with?"

"Ummm…" I wasn't exactly going to blurt out "the angel group." Maybe there was a "Martin group." I quickly looked around. All through the cabin, people seemed to be working on projects.

"The quilters are by the fire," said Zack, pointing with his violin bow. "The bakers are in the kitchen, the sign-makers are at the supper table, and the musicians are out in the yard. With the festival starting Friday, we don't have much time left to get ready."

"Hey, Zack, move your carcass out here!" somebody yelled from outside the window. "It's time for some 'Turkey in the Straw'!"

Turkey in the Straw

"Gotta go, Hannah. Catch you later!" Zack took off toward the door, his violin tucked under his arm.

I just stood there for a minute in the middle of all the music and quilt-making. *Turkey in the Straw?* What did *that* mean?

So here I was in this big, cozy log home. Handmade quilts were hanging on the walls. A fire was crackling in a huge stone fireplace. I could smell pies from the kitchen...so I decided to head that way.

The kitchen was full of jars of preserves, fresh-baked pies, and a bunch of busy women. Their hands were white with flour.

"Welcome, Hannah," said one of the bakers. "I'm Anne Megan's mom."

"She also happens to be just the *best* blueberry pie baker in all of West Virginia," said another lady, who was rolling out a crust on a big wood table.

"If you're looking for Anne Megan, she's upstairs," said her mom, pointing toward a staircase by the back door. "Take an apple with you, if you'd like." As she went back to her pie baking, I grabbed an apple from a bowl and headed upstairs.

So, I was in West Virginia! On the way up the stairs, I added a line to Katie in my journal:

> P.S. I'm in the Appalachian Mountains.
>
> Bye, H.

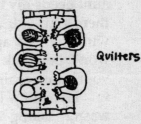

My balcony view

Quilters

At the top of the stairs was a balcony. Down below, I could see the quilters and sign-makers, busy as bees. So far, the big sign said:

SUMMERSTONE CREEK
FALL FESTIVAL
FRIDAY, SATU

sign-makers

They were still working on the "RDAY." I peeked in an open door across the hall. A girl was sitting at a computer that had a big lime green star on the screen.

"Hi! I said. "Are you Anne Megan?"

"*Pleeeease!*" she said, groaning. "You must have been talking to my mom. My name's Annie. Annie Jones. Megan is my middle name."

Annie at her computer

"I'm Hannah Martin," I said.

Annie was wearing a pale yellow sweatshirt that said UNIVERSITY OF PARIS on it. Her red hair was all curly and fell down almost to her waist.

"So, you must be here for the Fall Festival," said Annie. "Are you staying in one of our cabins?"

"I don't know," I told her. "I just got here."

"Well, I'm staying in a cabin tonight, since my aunt needs my bedroom—hey, come to think of it, there's an extra bed. You want to stay in there with me? I'd appreciate it, actually. That way I won't be stuck with my cousin Millie. What is your name again?"

"Hannah," I said, glad she wasn't asking any questions about where I'd come from. The people I meet on my angel missions almost never do. "And sure, I'll stay with you. Why not?"

"Great!" said Annie.

"What are you drawing on your computer screen?" I asked.

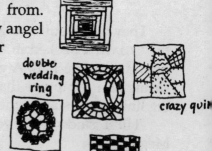

log cabin

double wedding ring

flower garden

crazy quilt

postage stamp

Annie's quilt designs

"It's a quilt," she said. I'm designing a new star pattern. Kind of like the one over there."

I looked over to where she was pointing. The entire wall was covered with bright printouts of circles, triangles, flowers, and squares.

"Are these all designs for quilts?" I asked.

"Yep," she said, getting up to show me. She pointed to a design like the one on the computer. "This is called a star pattern. Very traditional."

"I think it's beautiful," I said.

"I like inventing my own designs better. These are my favorites," she said, pointing to some watery, dreamy-colored patches. "They look like Monet's water lilies, don't they?"

They *did* look like water lilies. "What's this one?" I asked, pointing to a red-and-white one.

"That's the wedding band design. It's very popular." Annie had names for all the designs, so I wrote them down for Katie.

Out the window, I could see Zack in the yard playing that fast, happy music with some other musicians. There was a banjo, a guitar, and Zack on the violin.

"That's my brother, Zack, down there," said Annie.

"He plays the violin, huh?" I asked.

Annie giggled. "Don't let him hear you call it a violin. To him, it's a fiddle. He even named it: Valentine."

The music wasn't much like what I usually

heard at home. It was real lively. It made you want to tap your feet and dance around. A bunch of little kids were clapping along, having a really good time. I wanted to run downstairs and join them.

"I've got to finish this last design," Annie said. "You want to meet back downstairs when story-telling starts?"

"When is that?" I asked.

"Who knows?" said Annie. "Whenever the spirit moves them."

"Okay," I said. "See you." I wondered if Annie was the person I needed to help on my mission. Or was it Zack?

I went down to the yard and started clapping to the music. Each player took a turn, playing solo. Everybody whooped and cheered when Zack was done. He sure was one awesome fiddler.

Backyard musicians

"You got that first-place prize money wrapped up again this year, Zack!" somebody said.

Out of the corner of my eye, I saw a boy staring at Zack. His baseball cap was on backward, and he had grass stains and brown oil smeared on his jeans. He stood out because he was the only one who did not look happy. In fact, he had daggers in his eyes. He looked about sixteen—a high school version of Jimmy Fudge. Great, just what I needed.

I got a sinking feeling that this kid had something to do with my mission. So I started to walk toward him. The minute I did, he began chomping on some corn chips really loud.

"What are you looking at, fancy pants?" he said boldly.

Fancy pants? I tossed a cracker in my mouth. "Nothing," I said coolly. "Nothing at all."

He gave me a nasty look and jumped on an old dirt bike. As he sped off, I was left with a mouthful of dust.

"Thanks a lot!" I sputtered after him, choking.

"So I see you met Ben Turner," said Zack, coming up beside me. "He's a real toad."

"I noticed," I said. "What's he even doing here?"

"He wants to beat me out of the prize for playing fiddle on Friday night. It's two hundred dollars. He is a pretty good fiddler, if you can believe it."

"Is the fiddle contest part of the Fall Festival?"

"You bet it is!" said Zack. "Hey, did you taste the flapdoodle?" he asked.

"The *what* doodle?" I said.

"Here, you've got to try some." He spooned

blackberries with sugar sauce into a bowl and handed me a buttered biscuit. "Flapdoodle," he repeated. "You'll love it."

He was right. Flapdoodle is great. The music kept going while I tasted a little of everything on the table: corn bread, pink beans and ham, horse-radish pickles, apple pie, and molasses cookies. When I was totally stuffed, the sun started setting behind the mountains. Everybody headed inside.

"Time for some firelight tales," said Zack. "There'll probably be some scary ones tonight."

"Cool!" I said eagerly. "I love scary stories!"

In the living room, people were gathered by the big stone fireplace. A woman was standing in front of the fire, her face all shadowy as she told her tale.

"And when he opened his eyes he gasped in fear," she was saying, "as if he'd seen a ghost." Her voice was trembly and terrifying. When she said "ghost," it was "ghooooooo...sssssssst." For a minute, I thought I was getting a message from Lyra. But I wasn't.

Firelight tales

Annie leaned over to me. "It's the Pointing Finger story," she whispered. "It's about a guy who had his hand cut off in a mining accident."

"Because, floating before him," the storyteller continued, "the miner saw his own severed hand. It was glowing in the dark!"

Gross.

Each person took a turn at telling a story. Throughout the course of the night, I heard about headless miners wandering around in the mountains, phantom trains, horrible mining accidents, and children who came back to haunt their parents. By the time they finished, I was all creeped out. My skin was crawling, and I was jumpy.

Did I really need to hear this for my mission? I didn't think so. I kept watching for a word or sign from one of my angels. But so far, not a peep.

"Time to turn in, everybody," Annie's dad finally announced. "We've got a lot of work to do tomorrow to get ready for the festival."

It was dark when Annie and I stepped outside to go to the cabin. I mean, it was *really* dark. Like the inside of that cave on my last mission, in Mexico. Only we were outside in the open air. I felt spooked, just as if all those phantoms and headless creatures were hiding in the hills, waiting to grab me.

Chapter 3

The Outhouse Moon

Annie snatched up a lantern, and we headed out into the pitch dark.

"There's no electricity in the cabins," she said.

Just my luck! With my head full of spooky tales, the last thing I needed was no lights. I followed Annie down the stone steps of the path toward our cabin, constantly looking behind me for one of those headless miners.

As we walked, we could hear musicians still playing in a couple of cabins. Autumn leaves, dry and dead, rustled in the wind. The sky was black as coal, except for the stars, which went all the way down and touched the mountains. The moon was a little bone white wedge. It looked like a dead miner's grin.

Inside the cabin, there was a small woodstove and a bunk bed, covered with quilts. There were curtains on the windows and a collection of books on the dresser: *Little Women, Treasure Island, Arabian Nights*.

cozy inside

"You can have the top bunk," Annie said as she set the lamp on the table. It glowed all yellow and warm. Little beams of candlelight shone from the tiny holes of the lantern and threw a star pattern on the walls and ceiling. If it hadn't been for the firelight stories, I would have felt all snug and cozy in such a cool cabin.

"Did you make these quilts?" I asked Annie.

"I designed them," she said. "Then my mom, my grandma, and I stitched them together."

Wow! They were awesome! They were handmade, with scraps of every color. They'd been sewn into pictures of trees and log cabins and clouds.

"Here," she said, opening the drawer. "I have extra clothes you can borrow. We'll keep the fire stoked tonight. It's really chilly."

I found some red pj's while Annie got the woodstove going. We got all snuggled in bed under our quilts. I opened my journal and began writing.

Wednesday night

Dear Katie,

It's really, really dark here, and I'm staying in a little log
cabin. David would love all the books. You'd love the bunk
beds—they have handmade quilts. The coal mining
stories I heard are terrifying—I'll write one down later.
I don't know why I'm here yet. What do scary stories
and a fall festival have to do with my mission? I have to
go to the bathroom.

Bye, Hannah

It was true—I *did* need to go to the bathroom.
But I sure didn't feel like walking back to the
house in the pitch dark, especially in these long
red pj's.

"How long would it take to get back to the
house if I ran?" I asked Annie. "I have to use the
bathroom."

"The outhouse is closer," she replied.

"Outhouse?" I asked. Oh, no, say it ain't so! I
knew exactly what *that* was: one of those little
potty shacks with no plumbing.

"We almost never use it," said Annie. "My
dad keeps it because his grandfather built it
himself."

"So it's kind of a family heir-
loom, huh?" I asked.

Annie giggled. "Kind of. It
sounds like you're not too
thrilled about outhouses,

The outhouse

Hannah. I'll walk with you, if you want."

I'm always up for an adventure, but a cold, nasty outhouse, in my pj's, in the dark? I wasn't exactly jumping for joy. But what could I do? We slipped our boots on, grabbed the lantern and went back out into the dark night.

"Zack and I used to make up outhouse horror stories," Annie said, as we walked up a hill and past a lake. "We were positive that a pale creature lived in there—a slimy serpent who bathes in the light of the moon."

"Not another one!" I said. "I've had enough scary stories for one night."

"Okay," Annie said, laughing. "I'll wait here for you."

There was a crescent moon carved on the out-house door. The moonlight shone through it. Luckily, there wasn't a bathing serpent on the other side of the door. I'd almost half-expected one.

When Annie and I came back past the lake, the water was floating with stars, like a mirror of the sky.

"Hannah, look!" Annie whispered. "Something's weird with the stars!" She pointed to the middle of the lake. The stars in the Big Dipper were moving around. They finally straightened out and made an arrow.

"It's pointing back to our cabin!" I said. There was no doubt about it. It was a

Aurora's
arrow

message from another one of my angels, Aurora. We had to get back to the cabin, and quick.

We took off racing. The minute we got back to the cabin door, I felt it. Something just wasn't right.

"Somebody's been in here," I whispered.

Annie and I looked at each other, wide-eyed. Then she kicked the door open, and we jumped back against the log wall. We didn't hear a sound. Slowly, we moved toward the doorway and peeked in. The woodstove was still burning. Our stuff was where we'd left it. It didn't look like anything had been messed with.

One step at a time, we made our way inside. Annie checked under the bunk beds. I checked behind the dresser. There was nothing. Nobody.

Then, suddenly, Annie let out a scream.

"Hannah! Look at this!" she shrieked. She was pointing at the quilt from her bed. There was embroidery sewn onto one of the squares, right over the little red house with the smoking chimney. It was all glowing in the dark.

A message!

"It's the weirdest writing I've ever seen!" said Annie.

But I recognized the symbols right away—

Lorielle, Angel Number Three, had sent us a message! She always sends them in a special code. I dashed over to my backpack and pulled out my angel language decoder.

"What's that?" Annie asked. "What's going on?"

"I'll tell you in a minute!" I said. I wrote furiously, decoding Lori's message. When I finally translated the message, my mouth dropped open in shock.

"Tell me!" said Annie.

"Your brother...," I said. I read it again, just to make sure. I couldn't believe it.

"What?" cried Annie. *"What?"*

"It's your brother...Zack," I said. "He's been kidnapped!"

Chapter 4

Kidnapped!

"Kidnapped?" Annie yelped. "What are you talking about?"

"I don't know," I said. Lori's message hadn't told me much. All it said was that Zack had been kidnapped.

"Come on. We have to tell my mom and dad," said Annie, grabbing the lantern. She'd forgotten all about the decoder by now, thank goodness. She was out the door in a flash. It took us half the time to get back to the house, we were hurrying so fast.

Racing to tell Annie's parents

When we reached the house, Annie's parents were sitting on the front porch.

"Mom! Dad!" Annie yelled. "Somebody kidnapped Zack!"

22

They both looked at her like she was crazy.

"Anne Megan Jones," said her mom. "What dramatic story are you making up now?"

"We came back from the outhouse…" said Annie, all breathless.

"And the quilt on Annie's bed had stitching on it that wasn't there before," I added.

"But the stitches were weird. They had all these strange symbols, and they glowed in the dark, and…"

"I used a special decoder to translate the message, and…"

The more we talked, the crazier we must have sounded. Annie's mom and dad were staring at us like we had come down with some goofy sort of cabin fever.

"Slow down, girls," said Annie's dad.

"Come here and sit down," said her mom. "Have some hot apple cider." She poured us steaming mugs from a pot sitting on the table, and dropped a cinnamon stick in each.

Hot cider

"Now, girls," Annie's dad said, real slow and easy. He was trying to calm us down. "What makes you think Zack has been, uh, kidnapped?"

Annie and I looked at each other. We didn't have much to go on. Nobody had witnessed the kidnapping. There was no ransom note. Of course, *I* knew I could trust Lori's angel message.

But how could I explain that to them?

"Hannah told me," said Annie. Then there was silence all around, except for the chirping of the crickets.

All of a sudden, I felt like a jerk. The three of them were staring at me, waiting. I was sunk. There was nothing to say. No explanation I could give at all.

"I just *know*," I said in a small voice. It was all I could think of.

"Now, dear, those spooky stories can make you imagine all sorts of unnatural things," said Annie's mom, smiling at me. "When I was young, I *knew* there was a hand that lived under my bed, and I just *knew* it came crawling out at night to grab me by the neck." She laughed. "It was those darn ghost stories."

They were all laughing. What could I say?

"Annie, you know how Zack loves to ramble off into the hills sometimes," said Mrs. Jones. "He always comes home soon enough."

"Besides, he knows these hills like he knows his own name," said Mr. Jones. "Zack's got a lot of Huckleberry Finn in him. If he didn't go exploring, he just wouldn't be Zack."

Annie looked at me. "Maybe my brother went to his secret lookout campsite to practice his fiddle in private." She leaned over the corner of the porch and squinted out at the distant mountains.

"Look, Hannah!" she said, pointing. "Do you

see that little speck of light way up there in the hills? That's right about where Zack's hideout is."

I could see a tiny light shining in the dark.

Looking for Zack's light

"He camps out there a lot and never tells us where he's going," said Annie. "Sometimes he's there two or three times in a week. It's his favorite place to practice his fiddle."

I nodded. How could I explain to them that, even though the light was shining, Zack was still missing? I know my angel messages are always right. Even when they seem too incredible to believe. I just didn't know how to convince Annie and her parents.

"He'll be back tomorrow morning to show off his fancy fiddling to everybody," Mr. Jones said. He tried to stiffle a yawn.

"What you girls need now is a good night's sleep," Mrs. Jones added. "We still have a lot of preparation for the big weekend ahead."

Annie's parents got up and went into the house.

"Now scoot off to bed, you two," Mr. Jones said through the screen door.

Annie and I were left sitting in the dark, by the light of the lantern. "You don't believe Zack's been kidnapped, do you?" I asked Annie.

She looked at me apologetically. "You can see his light up in the hills, Hannah," she said. "And nobody has a reason to kidnap him."

I understood why she didn't believe me. I couldn't blame her for wanting to believe that her brother was all right. But how was I going to prove that my angel message was true?

Suddenly, I felt a familiar tug on my hair. I knew it wasn't a headless miner, and I knew it wasn't some bodiless hand. Thank goodness!

It was my guardian angel, Demi, right there on Annie's front porch.

Chapter 5

The Angel Plan

"I'll be right back," I said. "I'm going to the bathroom." That's always the best excuse when Demi wants to talk to me, because it's private.

"But you just went to the outhouse," said Annie, frowning.

"I know," I said. "But I'll be right back anyhow." I dashed into the house, found the bathroom, and shut the door. I looked in the mirror. Just as I suspected, my hair was sticking up where Demi had tugged at it.

Demi at my hair again

"Are you there, Demi?" I whispered.

"I'm here, Hannah," came her voice. Demi definitely makes her presence obvious when I need her. But only obvious to me. So I can't talk to her with

27

other people around, or they'll think I'm talking to thin air.

"What am I going to do?" I asked her, patting my hair back into place.

"What do *you* think you should do?" she asked.

Darn! She's always making me think for myself. She never gives me easy answers.

"I have no idea," I moaned. "I know Zack's been kidnapped, but nobody believes me. They think it's my overactive imagination."

She tugged at my hair again. I hate when she does that. And she does it a lot!

"So they think Zachary is at his secret lookout, practicing his music, right?" asked Demi.

"Right," I said.

"So what if you hike up to his lookout with Annie, and—"

"She'll see he's not there!" I finished. "Perfect!"

"Good thinking, Hannah!" Demi told me. "You're on your own now."

"Wait, Demi, wait!" I said. "Don't leave yet! Tell me where Zack is!"

All I could hear was silence. But just when I thought she had left, I felt her smoothing my hair back in place.

"Demi?" I asked. "Are you still here?"

"I'm here," she said. "But you know I can't just tell you where Zachary is. You have to—"

"Figure it out for myself!" I finished, sighing. "I know. So can you give me a hint? Just a little one?"

"You'll be receiving clues along the way," she said mysteriously. "Just keep your eyes open."

"What about the first clue? Can you give me the first clue?" I pleaded.

"Of course not," said Demi. "I think you know where to start, don't you?"

"Zack's hideaway?" I asked.

"My brilliant girl!" exclaimed Demi. "Look for a note there."

"A ransom note from the kidnappers?" I asked. But Demi was gone.

A note. Okay, I could work with that. I went back out onto the porch.

"Annie," I said. "Do me a favor, okay? Just to humor me, let's go up to Zack's lookout and make sure he's there."

Annie looked at me sadly, like she was worried for me and my wild imagination.

"Okay, Hannah," she said. "But we can't go looking for him in the middle of the night. It's too dangerous. And it's a long way."

"Can we leave first thing in the morning, then?" I asked. If I had my choice, we would have left right this very minute. But Annie was right—I didn't really want to go traipsing through the mountains in the pitch dark.

"Okay," said Annie. "As long as we're back

before Friday noon. That's when the festival starts."

"Great," I said. That gave us two whole days. With the help of my angels, I knew we could find Zack and get him back in time.

"We'll leave at first light," said Annie. "Let's pack up some things while we're here. And I'll leave a note for my parents. They won't be too happy, but at least they won't worry about us."

We tiptoed into the kitchen. The cupboards had jars full of dried apples, bananas, raisins, and nuts, which we packed up for a trail mix. Annie grabbed homemade bread and apple butter, strawberry roll-ups, and beef jerky. We took two canteens and filled them with water and then put everything into a bag.

Kitchen Cupboards

Then we went upstairs. Annie stuffed into her backpack, trying not to wake anyone up. I spotted a small tent rolled up in the closet.

"Should we take that tent?" I whispered.

"I really don't think we'll need it, Hannah," said Annie.

"Just in case," I said.

She strapped the tent onto the bottom of her backpack. We headed back to the cabin. This time, it didn't feel as far away. I was getting used to following the hilly paths in the dark.

"I can't imagine who would ever want to kidnap Zack," said Annie on the way. "I bet you we'll find him right there, up at his lookout, safe and sound."

"Maybe," I said.

"Besides, suppose the very worst thing did happen," Annie said, "and Zack *was* kidnapped by some creepy guy. He'd be way too much trouble for anybody to handle, anyway."

"That's good," I said. "Is he kind of a problem?"

"Not at all. He's just hardheaded. Independent," said Annie. "And he's always playing that fiddle. I don't think any kidnappers could stand to have him for too long."

I laughed. It sounded like something my dad would say about me. Except the fiddle part.

As soon as we got back, I dumped everything from my backpack onto the floor. Inside was yellow rain gear (just like I had in Australia), my flashlight, my flute, my colored pencils, a rope, a compass, and twenty-five dollars in three bills. And a little instrument thing of some sort.

"Do you know what this is?" I asked Annie.

"A pedometer. It tells you how far you've walked when you're hiking. Can I borrow it?" she asked.

"Sure," I said. I loaded my stuff back into my

pack and threw in a sweatshirt and flannel shirt that Annie let me borrow.

When we got into our bunk beds, Annie blew out the lantern. I could hardly settle down, I was so excited. My first kidnapping mission. *Who would want to kidnap Zack? I wondered. And how do we un-kidnap him?*

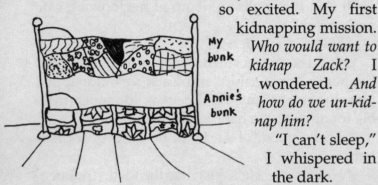

My bunk

Annie's bunk

"I can't sleep," I whispered in the dark.

"I'll tell you a bedtime story," said Annie. "That always works for me."

Nobody had told me a bedtime story since I was about eight. It sounded like a great idea.

"The Blue Flame," Annie announced, like an official storyteller, "is about a boy who saw a blue light in a mine shaft. He kept going deeper and deeper into the dark, following the light. Rats were scurrying around, bats were flying overhead…"

Great, just what I needed. Another ghost story.

Chapter 6

Off with Annie

"Hannah, it's dawn!" yelled Annie.

As I sprang up to a sitting position, my head hit the ceiling. Whoops, I'd forgotten I was on a bunk bed. After I finished rubbing my head, I jumped down from the bunk. Annie and I quickly grabbed all the stuff we had packed the night before and headed out. It was time to go to Zack's lookout.

The sky was all orange and pink. The trees were bright fall colors and I could smell the leaves. This really was a beautiful place.

Annie led the way to Zack's hideout—up a mountainside and down into a valley.

"We call this a holler," said Annie, as we hiked down into the valley.

"A what?" I asked.

"A holler. You know, a hollow. A place

between the mountains where it's all open and flat. It's a good place to live, because the wind doesn't blow so hard down here."

The holler was red with sumac.

"Is this sumac poisonous?" I asked Annie.

We checked it out. The plants had red berries.

"No. Just regular," said Annie. "Poison sumac has droopy white berries."

"I know," I told her. "We have sumac in Wisconsin, too." I told her about Jimmy Fudge's poison sumac episode, and she howled, thinking it was so funny.

Then she told me about ramps.

"Ramps?" I asked. "Like wheelchair ramps?"

"No, not that kind!" she said, laughing. "In West Virginia, ramps are vegetables, like the wild onions that grow in the spring. If you eat them raw, you smell so bad that teachers send you home from school. Ben Turner is famous for gorging himself on ramps so he can disgust everyone around him."

Then Annie suddenly pointed toward the woods. I turned around and saw three deer,

The three deer

with white tails, wandering around in the trees. I'm pretty good at seeing wildlife, but Annie was unbelievable. She could see birds and bugs and chipmunks way before I did.

Zack's hideout was a lot farther away than it looked. We couldn't just go in a straight path—we had to hike up and down lots of hills.

"Let's stop for water," Annie said, after we'd been walking for almost an hour.

"Great!" I said. I collapsed on a big rock in the sun. My feet were already aching. I was so thirsty that I gulped down almost all the water in my canteen.

"Here, I'll get you more," said Annie. "There's an artesian well over there."

"A what?" I asked.

"An artesian well—one that comes out of the ground," said Annie. "It's just a few feet away."

There was a pool of clear, clean water, with bubbles coming up from the middle. Annie dipped our canteens in and filled them up. *Wow, artesian wells are pretty handy*, I thought.

As I watched, a chubby little raccoon waddled out of the woods and dipped something into the water, right next to Annie.

"She's washing an apple core," Annie whispered. The raccoon washed it very carefully, taking her time. I guess she wanted to make sure all the people germs were gone before she ate it. Before she waddled away, she turned around and looked at us for a couple of seconds.

Our special raccoon

"Did you take a close look at that raccoon?" Annie asked.

"Sort of," I said.

"She had a little mark on her paw, shaped like a heart." I had never seen a raccoon with a birthmark before. That was one cool raccoon.

We moved on and finally got to Zack's hideout. There was a small tent and a fire pit nestled beside a gigantic rock jutting out over the tree tops.

"Look!" shouted Annie. "Zack's lantern is still burning."

I tiptoed over to the edge of the rock to get the lantern. The countryside spread out below me for miles around. It looked like one of Annie's quilts, with square patches of red and orange and yellow and green. In the distance were blue, hazy mountains.

Zack's hideout

"No wonder Zack loves coming here!" I said. But Annie wasn't listening.

"Hey, Zack!" she was yelling. "You have visitors!" There was no answer. I wasn't surprised.

Annie unzipped the tent flap and poked her head in. Then she pulled it right back out.

"Hannah, come here!" she said, sounding scared. "Somebody's messed up Zack's stuff."

I dashed over and pulled the flap aside to look in. The tent was in shambles. The sleeping bag was in a lumpy pile, and there were clothes and magazines everywhere. Zack's fiddle was nowhere in sight. I got a chill up my spine to the top of my head.

"Something terrible's happened," said Annie. Her eyes were starting to tear up.

"Zack usually keeps his stuff real neat," she said. "Somebody was definitely here. Do you think they...do you think they...hurt him?" she asked, choking back tears.

I put my arm around Annie's shoulder. "We're going to find him," I said. "I swear."

"Who would want to kidnap Zack?" she whimpered. "And *why?*"

"I don't know," I said. "But we'll get him back, I promise. Let's look for a note."

"A note?" she asked, puzzled.

"You know, like a ransom note or something. I bet there's one here." Of course, I *knew* that there was—Demi had told me so.

I crawled into the tent and shuffled through Zack's things. Annie looked around outside.

"Hannah!" she hollered. "I found something!"

I scrambled out of the tent. In the dirt, somebody had scratched an image with a stick. It looked like this: Fork note

Chapter 7

Baloney Breath

"Do you think Zack drew this?" asked Annie.

"I don't think Zack would have known where he was going if he was kidnapped," I said.

"True," Annie agreed. "Maybe it was his kidnapper."

"We should probably follow it and see where it takes us."

"But if the kidnapper did it, this could be a trap," said Annie. She *was* making a good point. But how could I tell her I knew it wasn't a trap?

"I still think we should give it a try," I said. I gave the picture another look. "There's a line that turns into three, like a fork," I said.

Annie twisted a strand of hair around her finger, thinking. "A fork..." she mused. "It can only be the fork in the road ahead."

"How far away is it?" I asked.

Fork in the road

"About half a mile," said Annie.

"Well, let's go!"

We zipped up Zack's tent, blew out his lantern, and headed back down to the main trail. I could tell Annie was concentrating on something while we hiked. It was like sparks were flying from her brain— wheels turning.

"I know who did it," she said suddenly. "I know who kidnapped Zack."

"Who?" I asked.

"Baloney Breath."

"*Who?*" I asked again.

"Benjamin Seth, Baloney Breath," she chanted. "It's what we called him when he was little. His mother calls him by his full name: Benjamin Seth Turner."

"Hey, I saw him at your house yesterday!" I said. "The guy with the stained jeans who zoomed off on his dirt bike! The ramps guy! Does his breath really smell like baloney?"

"No. It's just that every dopey word that comes out of his mouth is a bunch of baloney," replied Annie.

"So why would Ben kidnap Zack?" I asked.

"Ben really wants to win the fiddling contest on Friday night," Annie said. "He took second place last year behind Zack, and you should have heard him carry on about how much better he was than Zack 'the Hack' Jones afterwards. The baloney was really spewing after he lost, and I don't think he wants it to happen again."

"So he figures if he can keep Zack from playing, he'll win first prize this year?" I asked. I was beginning to get a clear picture of my mission.

"Exactly!" said Annie. "He is so low-down and dirty!"

She was right—this Baloney Breath guy sounded like a true jerk.

"Do you really think we can rescue Zack by ourselves?"

"I guess that depends," I said. "How dangerous is this Baloney Ben guy?"

"I wouldn't really call him dangerous," said Annie. "He's ignorant and bullheaded, but he's about as dangerous as a moose in a mineshaft."

"Good," I said. "I can handle stupid, but dangerous is another thing."

"One night," Annie continued, "Ben bragged that he was going to tip over our outhouse. So Zack and I spied on him, hoping that he'd use it first. And he did. So guess what we did?"

"What?" I asked.

"We locked him in!"

"So did he turn over the outhouse?" I asked.

"No, he just howled like a wounded bear until we let him out. Then he ran home, holding his nose all the way," said Annie, laughing.

Baloney Breath was beginning to sound more

and more like Jimmy Fudge.

"Does Baloney Breath have a secret hideout of his own?" I asked.

Annie shook her head. "If he does, it's *really* a secret hideout," she said. "Because I have no idea where it could be. I guess our best bet is to head for the fork."

"And see if there's another clue there," I added.

Annie grabbed a long, straight branch from underneath a fallen tree. It was almost as tall as she was, very sturdy, and had a little knob toward the top.

Our walking sticks

"A natural walking stick," she said. "The hiking gets tougher as we get toward that fork, so it's nice to have something to lean on. You want one, too?"

"Yeah," I said, glancing around. I picked up a crooked branch, and the minute I leaned on it, it broke in half. Annie giggled.

"You need something sturdier than that," she said. We kept our eyes peeled as we continued hiking. Pretty soon, I spotted a thick, gnarly branch, taller than me.

"Perfect!" said Annie. "We can also use it to crack somebody over the head if they get rambunctious."

"Like Baloney Breath, you mean?" I asked.

"You got it!" she said.

"So tell me everything about you," said Annie out of the blue. "Just so I know who I'm traveling with, you know?"

"Well, let's see," I said. How do you tell somebody everything all at once? "I was born on April Fool's Day, I have a mom, a dad, a dog named Frank—"

"No, not that stuff!" said Annie, exasperated. "Important stuff. Like, take me for instance—my favorite color is apple green, which is the color of the leaves in April. And I love weeping willow trees, because they keep growing even though they look so sad."

Annie

"Oh, okay! I get it!" I said. Annie sure had a way of talking. Her words were poetic. "I have glow-in-the-dark stars all over my ceiling. And I love drawing with my colored pencils."

"I dream of living in Paris someday, on the left bank of the River Seine," said Annie, "with a silky white cat named Claudette."

"I write everything down in my journal," I told her. "I love lowland gorillas. And I believe in angels."

Me

Just when I said that, we arrived at the fork in the trail. It parted into three paths, just like the clue showed us.

Annie pointed out each way. "This path winds down to Summerstone Creek," she said. "This one goes to the top of the mountain. And that one veers over to the strip mine."

"So which way do we go?" I asked.

"Your guess is as good as mine," said Annie. She sat down on a tree stump and pulled the canteen from her shoulder. "Here, have a swig," she said.

I glanced around. I was sure we'd find another note.

Just then, a raccoon ambled toward us from behind a bush. She silently circled Annie's tree stump. Then she tramped across my feet and scurried down the center path of the fork. And as she looked back, I swear she stared at me right in the eye. It was as if she was telling us to follow her.

Chapter 8

Headless Mountains?

"Did you see the mark?" cried Annie.

"Sure did!" I said.

"A gray heart, right in the middle of her left paw!"

"It's our raccoon!" I shouted.

Annie was already on her feet. We hurried down the middle fork as our raccoon friend disappeared into the brush as suddenly as she had appeared.

On the way to the strip mine, we saw so many wild mushrooms. They were sprouting up everywhere, under the leaves and between the trees. Annie bent down and picked a couple. She rubbed off the black dirt.

"Hungry?" she asked.

"Not hungry enough to die," I said. I remembered Ms. Crybaby's lecture about poisonous mushrooms.

"My grandpa taught me how to tell the good mushrooms from the poisonous ones. Rule number one is: If you're not absolutely, positively sure, don't even think about eating them."

"Are you absolutely, positively sure about these mushrooms?" I asked.

"Absolutely, positively," she answered.

"What if you eat a poisonous one?" I asked.

"Well, I once heard a story about a big, burly miner who took the tiniest taste of the wrong mushroom. In seconds, his throat closed up, his eyes bugged out, and he fell over dead, right on the spot."

"That's horrible!" I said, shivering.

"They say mushrooms sprouted up all over his body in the blink of an eye," Annie continued. "By the time help came, you couldn't find his body anywhere because there was only a lumpy mound of mushrooms."

Poor miner !

R.I.P.

"Is that a true story?" I asked.

"Who knows?" she said. "But it's like they say: Truth is stranger than fiction."

I looked down at the mushroom in my hand and shuddered. It was gold-orange and shaped like a chubby little umbrella. I waited for Annie to try her mushroom first. She popped it in her mouth. Her eyes didn't bug out or anything.

Non-poisonous golden chanterelle

(They grow on separate stems)

"I know what I'm talking about," she said. "These are called golden chanterelles. They're delicious—and safe." I tried a little taste. It was very different from the mushrooms I've had from the stores. This one was peppery and really good.

"How about this one, Annie?" I asked reaching down to pick another.

"Throw that far away!" Annie yelled. "That's a jack-o'-lantern, the most poisonous mushroom in this area!" I quickly did as she said. I couldn't believe how good Annie was at identifying the mushrooms. It wasn't like the jack-o'-lantern was bright red with white dots on it or anything.

Poisonous Jack-o'-lantern

(their stems grow together)

To me, it looked exactly like the golden chanterelle. I had no idea how she told the two apart.

"Will I get a rash from touching it?" I asked, thinking about Jimmy Fudge and the sumac.

"I don't know," said Annie. "I've never touched one."

I wiped my fingers on my pant leg, splashed some canteen water on them, and wiped again. A strange feeling began to creep up my spine.

"Do you get the feeling we're being watched?" I asked, looking around.

"I don't know," said Annie. Her eagle eyes

scanned the woods. "I don't see anyone."

"I'm keeping an eye out," I said, as we hiked on. "I just got a really weird feeling that we aren't alone."

Soon we reached a spot where the mountains didn't have tops. I'm not kidding. No tops—can you believe that! The peaks were completely flat, like some alien ship had leveled them with a big machine. They looked really strange.

Headless Mountains

"Why don't these mountains have tops?" I asked.

"Strip mining," said Annie. "They cut the tops off to get the coal from inside. Isn't it ugly?"

"Really ugly. Who said they could do that?" I asked.

"The mining companies own those mountains," said Annie. "Some things they can't do, but they can slice off the tops to get the coal out."

"How can anyone own a whole mountain?" I asked. I was thinking about my friend George back in Australia, who said his people believe nobody owns the land. It belongs to everyone.

Below all the chopped-off mountains, there was a big industrial-looking area.

"That's the strip mine," said Annie. Enormous machines were making a terrible racket, and dust was flying everywhere. I covered my eyes to keep out the grit.

"Come this way," said Annie.

I followed her around the side of the strip mine, where we walked from the hill right onto the roof of a metal shed.

"What do we do now?" I asked. I was keeping my eyes open for another message. But I didn't find one, yet.

"Let's think about this," said Annie. "Maybe somebody here has seen Zack. But we should be careful who we ask, because there's no telling who's in cahoots with Ben."

Suddenly, she grabbed my head and pushed me down onto the roof. We lay stretched out, like two alley cats. The sound of a buzzing motor approached.

Two cats on the tin roof

"Speak of the devil!" whispered Annie. "It's Ben Turner!"

We crawled out to the edge, still crouched down, so we could spy. Down below, a kid pulled up on a dirt bike. It was Ben, all right, dirty jeans and all. But instead of his baseball cap, he was wearing a purple bandanna tied around his head, biker-style.

"I knew it! That's Zack's lucky bandanna!" Annie whispered. "He always keeps it tied around his pant leg."

I gulped, trying to keep quiet as Ben rested his bike against a pile of rusty junk. He swaggered into the garage below us. We quickly pulled our heads out of sight.

"Hey, Ben!" somebody said.

"Hey, Willy boy!" said Ben. He was yelling over the noisy machines. "I need to pick up the tapes for my tape player. And they better be right where I left them, Willy boy, or some grease monkey mechanic is gonna be hurtin' big time."

"Give it up, Baloneymeister. They're over by the tools, against that wall," said Willy. "What are ya doing? Taping your fiddle music for the contest?"

"Yep," answered Ben. "I'm gonna fine-tune my wondrous style and play it back to see how great I sound."

"Think you're gonna beat out Zack Jones this year?" Willy asked, chuckling.

"I have a funny feeling that I might just beat little Hack this year!" Ben bragged.

"That'll be the day!" said Willy.

"You all might be real surprised!" called Ben, climbing onto his bike with the tapes in hand. "That two-hundred-dollar prize is as good as in my pocket on Friday night!" He hollered "Yahoo!" as he took off through the trees, leaving behind a cloud of smoke.

"He's headed west," whispered Annie. "He's not going back to town."

"Where's he going?" I whispered back.

"There's nothing that way but abandoned houses," said Annie. "Maybe he's got Zack locked up in one of them! But the only problem is, there are so many houses that it's like a whole ghost town."

"We'll find out where Zack is," I said. I knew there'd be another angel note soon enough.

"I don't know," said Annie. "The town is so big, it's like looking for a tiny needle in a giant haystack."

Chapter 9

Clues Three, Four, and S'more

Of course, Annie had no idea we had angels to help us find that needle in the haystack. I wondered which of my angels would show up next. If it was a note, it might be Lori. But Aurora had sent the star message in the lake (and maybe the raccoon), so I'd have to keep my eyes open for her, too.

In the junk pile

The minute Ben left, we climbed down the rocks to follow him. Annie leaped and landed by the junk pile. I jumped down beside her. We ducked behind the junk so Willy wouldn't see us. Old tires, twisted wires, and big rusted machine parts were stacked high. Some old license plates were nailed onto the fence.

Annie pointed to the plates. One read: ILV10SE. We silently giggled once we figured out that it meant "I Love Tennessee." Another said: URAQT, which meant: "You Are a Cutie." But there was one plate that was blue with clouds and had no state name. It looked completely different from all the others. It read:

My mouth dropped open as I figured out what it said.

"Go west two miles," I whispered to Annie.

Her eyebrows shot up in disbelief. After a second, she crept off down the road where Ben had gone. I followed behind her. Once we were out of Willy's sight, we stood straight up.

"Two miles west is probably right where Ben went," said Annie. "Those notes are incredible. Where are they coming from?"

I figured now was as good a time as any to tell her about the angels. So I gave it a try.

"Remember when we got the kidnapping note?" I said. "I pulled out a decoder to translate it."

"Yeah, what *was* that wheel thing you were turning?" said Annie.

"It's an angelic language decoder," I said. "Sometimes I get messages that need decoding, like the one on the license plate."

"You get them from *angels?*" asked Annie.

"Yes," I said. "Real angels."

"Hmmm...angels," said Annie. She twirled a strand of her red hair. I could tell she'd have to think about this one for a while. I guess it's not every day that you find out angels are helping you.

We could see Ben's tire tracks along the way. Since he went off-road, we had to hike over hills and through trees and we got all scratched and worn out. Well, at least *I* did. I guess Annie was used to mountain treks, because she looked exactly the same as when we started.

"Hey, Annie, why are all the houses abandoned?" I asked out of curiosity.

"Because of the strip mining," she said. "When they blast dynamite to behead those mountains, heaps of ashes and debris run down onto the houses."

"So people leave?" I asked. "They move out?"

"That's right," said Annie. "The air gets so full of dust that it's hard for them to breathe."

"That's terrible," I said.

"I know. And some of those families have been there since the 1800s," she said. "Now they're forced to leave the land where they grew up and find another place to live."

"That's really sad," I said.

"Two miles," Annie quickly said, checking our pedometer.

"You're such a mountaineer," I said.

"You have to be if you're going to travel this far into the woods," she said. "Now what? Do you think there's another note?"

We searched the area.

"I don't see or hear anything. How about you?" I asked.

Before Annie could answer, a familiar raccoon stepped out from a clump of wildflowers and sat down right on my foot.

"It's her again! It's the same raccoon we saw by the artesian spring! And at the fork!" Annie said, all amazed.

Sure enough, the raccoon had that little gray heart shape on her left paw! She circled around us and then pushed two twigs onto the path. The twigs made an X.

"This could be Aurora at work!" I exclaimed. "One of my angels!"

Annie didn't say anything. I guess she was still pondering the angel idea.

"What does the X mean?" she said, finally.

X marks the spot

It was then I noticed a circle of rocks, filled with ashes.

"We're right in the middle of a campsite!" I said.

"And none too soon," Annie added. "The sun is starting to set. I'd say this is as far as we should go today."

"I agree," I said.

"So do you think our raccoon friend will put the tent up for us?" Annie teased.

But when we turned around, the raccoon was gone. Once again, she had vanished into the trees.

"You know, my friend David brings his ferret when we go camping with my dad," I told Annie. "He has this little ferret-size tent that Squirt fits into perfectly."

"Squirt?" Annie asked, confused.

"Oh, that's the ferret's name," I replied. "He's real cute."

Annie shook her head. "You have remarkable friends," she said, laughing. "Ferrets and angels."

She raised the tent, and I drove the stakes in with a rock. I spread out our sleeping bags and Annie made a fire. By the time we were finished setting up camp, it was twilight.

"What's it like up in Wisconsin?" Annie asked, as we sat by the fire.

"It's a lot like here," I said. "But no big mountains." I had pulled out my flute and was playing a few notes.

Annie started to sing: "Hush, little baby, don't say a word."

"Papa's gonna buy you a mockingbird," I played along on the flute.

"And if that mockingbird don't sing..." Annie continued. But then she looked down at the ground, sadly. "Zack loves that tune," she said. "He used to play it to me when I was little and couldn't sleep."

Her voice began to break, and her eyes got a little watery.

"We'll find him, Annie," I promised.

"I've got to keep busy so I don't think about Ben Turner and Zack," she said suddenly. She began to pull out the food we'd brought from the kitchen.

I opened up my journal.

Thursday evening

Dear Katie,

We're camping in the middle of nowhere. There's a fog over the mountains that makes them look dreamy and blue. We have chocolate bars, graham crackers, and marshmallows— we're going to make s'mores over the fire. By the way, that was a really good idea of yours to have me keep a journal— I really like writing you notes from Blue Mountain. That's what I call this place, anyway.

Later, Hannah

Chapter 10⊙

Queens of the Universe

Annie suddenly stood up, stretching. "Okay. We need to do something fun," she announced. "Just you and me."

I'm *always* ready for something fun. But it seemed like such an awfully serious time right now. I mean, here we were deep in the woods, in the middle of the dark, searching for Annie's kidnapped brother. It wasn't exactly a fun situation.

"How can we have fun when Zack's being held hostage?" I asked.

"We've done all the work we can for tonight," she said. "It's time for us to kick back a little. Besides, I'd like to get my mind off it for a second or two."

"Okay, let's have some fun," I agreed, closing my journal. "What should we do?"

Annie thought for a minute. "I've got it!" she

finally said, as she fished around in her pack. First she brought out a flashlight and turned it on. Then she pulled out a tiny bottle of pale pink nail polish.

"Dawn Rose," Annie read from the label. "Let's do our toenails!"

"Okay," I said. "Pedicures!" We sat down and pulled off our shoes. Our feet were *filthy*.

"We can't put nail polish on dirty feet!" I said.

"Let's go down to the stream," said Annie. "Bring your socks."

We tiptoed over stones and twigs. It kind of hurt, but I felt like an adventurous mountaineer. We each sat on a rock and dipped our feet in the water.

"It's freezing!" I screamed. Annie agreed. It was really cold, but we kept our feet in until all the dirt washed off. Then we dried them off with our socks.

"Now," said Annie. "Let's take some twigs and put them between our toes! Then we won't get polish on our pinkies."

Toe twigs

"Good thinking," I agreed.

I picked up ten twigs to stick between my toes. Actually, I realized even though I have ten toes, I only needed eight twigs for the spaces in between. I guess I'd never really thought about that before.

After the toe twigs were all set, we took turns

painting each other's toenails. We may have been all rumpled and dirty, but once we were done painting, our feet looked fabulous.

"Now let's make necklaces," said Annie.

My nature necklace

While our toenails dried, we reached around us and picked up tiny pine cones and leaves, and twigs and berry clusters.

"I have a needle in my backpack," said Annie. "Let's go back and finish our necklaces."

I touched my nail polish to make sure it was dry before putting on my socks. It was. We tiptoed back to the campsite. Annie tapped me on the shoulder and whispered, "Now we're having fun, right?" I couldn't help but smile.

Once we sat back down by the fire, Annie took out her needle and thread, and we sewed through the thin stuff and tied on the heavy stuff. Pretty soon, we had our very own original nature necklaces.

"This is so cool," I said, tying mine around my neck. I pulled my socks back off. Now I looked like a model—my Dawn Rose toenails and a nature necklace.

"One final touch!" Annie announced. "Crowns!"

She started pulling leaves off a maple tree by our campsite.

"Just take the leaves that are the most beautiful," she instructed.

I began sorting through red ones, green ones, red *and* green ones. They looked really pretty by flashlight. There were so many to choose from, too. Soon I had twelve big maple leaves.

"Here's what you do," said Annie, sitting cross-legged in the grass. "Stick the stem of one leaf into the end of another. Do it with all your leaves until they become a chain."

My maple leaf crown

I did just that. I was careful not to make the holes too big, or the stem would pull back out. Then Annie took her chain of leaves and wrapped it around her head. She stuck the last stem into the end leaf to make it stay.

"I'm Queen of the Universe!" she yelled, jumping to her feet.

Annie was right. This *was* fun! I finished my crown and jumped up, too. I felt like a barefoot Dawn Rose Queen.

"No, *I'm* Queen of the Universe!" I hollered. I stretched my arms out and tried to put a snooty, regal look on my face.

Annie threw her arms out, too, blocking my face with one of her hands.

"No!" she yelled.

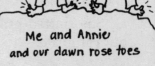

Me and Annie
and our dawn rose toes

"*I'm* Queen of the Universe!" She climbed up onto a rock and stood on the top. She turned with her arms still out, like she owned the streams and the trees and all of the blue mountains.

I ran over and knocked right into her. "Did you hear that? We're *both* the Queens of the Universe!" I shouted.

"Hey, mountains!" yelled Annie. "We're the Queens of the Universe!"

We kept giggling and shouting and carrying on, making a whole bunch of noise in the quiet forest.

"Hey, trees!" I yelled. "I'm Quee—" Then I stopped dead.

Down below, right in front of our tent, I heard a rumble and a crash. There was something fumbling around in our stuff, devouring our chocolate bars, graham crackers, and marshmallows.

Guess what had found our s'mores? A BEAR!

Chapter 11

Big Ol' Fur Belly

I froze with my arms up, still wearing my crown. I was so scared that I felt as stiff as a statue, and I'm sure I didn't look like a very regal one. I felt like being Queen of the Universe had been my last act on earth. Or actually, I felt like meeting this bear was *about to be* my last act on earth. I'd never been so close to a bear.

I knew from camping with my dad that you're supposed to make a lot of noise to warn the bears that you're around. Then they'll stay away. But it was too late. This bear was already in our campground, eating our treats.

"Annie!" I hissed through my clenched teeth. "It's a bear." I didn't move my mouth at all when I talked. I felt like a ventriloquist.

Annie stopped hollering and turned to look.

"Oh, no!" she cried. "Our s'mores!"

She didn't look particularly terrified. I inched over beside her, trembling.

Fur Belly in our s'mores

"What should we do?" I asked in my frozen dummy voice.

"Nothing," she said, calmly. "He'll go away when he's done feasting."

"Aren't you scared?" I asked.

"Nah, not really. Look how far away we are," she said.

I didn't feel far away at all. Actually, I felt like our noses were pressed together.

"The bears are active right now," said Annie. "They're eating everything they can get their paws on to get ready for hibernation."

"So they can go to sleep on full bellies?"

"Yep," said Annie. "Do you know what's the last thing a bear eats before it crawls into its cave to sleep?"

"Is this gonna be a joke?" I asked.

Happy hibernater

"No, it's for real. They tear a hunk of fur off their bellies. Then they swallow it to stop up their digestive systems."

"What? That bear will go to sleep with a belly full of fur?"

"That's right. He's a big ol' fur belly," said Annie.

I giggled. *Big ol' fur belly*. The name made him sound a little friendlier, even if he *was* fifty times bigger than my dog, Frank, and had huge teeth, too!

So we just waited up on our rock until the big ol' fur belly finished every last bite of our s'mores and peacefully lumbered away. Then we went back down to the campsite, making noise all the way. I checked around to make sure our bear didn't have any buddies following close behind.

"Time to turn in," said Annie.

"Good idea," I agreed. I didn't want to hang out and wait for another bear to stop by for a visit. Or worse, a mountain lion. So we cleaned up all our food to the very last crumb and zipped ourselves inside the tent.

By the light of the lantern, I wrote down my clues.

1. Fork in road: 3 paths
2. Middle trail to strip mine: raccoon
3. GOW2MI: license plate
4. X marks the campsite: raccoon

Goodnight notes

"What are you writing, Hannah?" Annie asked.

"Just our clues so far," I answered. I showed her the page. She was all quiet for a minute.

"I wish I were a writer," she said. "How do you just keep writing and writing like that?"

"I love to keep track of everything," I said. "And draw pictures of what I see."

Annie yawned and crawled into her sleeping bag. I jotted another quick note to Katie, about the bear, and Annie, and the dark night around me here in the Appalachian Mountains.

"Good night, Katie," I finished the note.

owl

I blew out the lantern. An owl hooted. I silently asked my angels to watch over Zack and keep him safe and sound through this dark night.

"Keep us safe, too," I added.

Chapter 12

My Stolen Heart

It was freezing when I woke up. I pulled my sleeping bag tightly around me and looked around.

Annie was gone.

But before I began to panic, I figured that she had simply gotten up early and gone to start a fire or something. I thought I'd write down my dreams, which had been full of poisonous mushrooms dangling from bony miners' fingers.

I stuck my hand into my backpack.

It was gone! My notebook was gone! *Now* I began to panic. Had Annie taken it?

Inside that notebook were all my angel ideas, my thoughts about Annie, my notes to Katie. It's one thing to show my notebook to Katie, whom I trust completely and absolutely.

Nightmare

But it's another to have somebody you don't know that well take it from you and read all your secrets.

Me, fuming

Thinking about it started to get me really mad. Not only had she stolen my journal, but she had stolen my heart, too. My face was really hot and I was red and seething. Even my blood felt funny, like it was jumpy or something.

My camping hair →

I threw open the sleeping bag and stormed out of the tent. At first I didn't want to see Annie. I looked around, remembering the bear. No sign of anything but a few chipmunks skittering around searching for breakfast, and a fire that Annie had started.

"Hannah!" Annie called from above. I looked up, and there she was sitting on the branch of a tree with *my* notebook! She had it open like it was the morning paper. I couldn't believe she could be so insensitive.

"What are you doing with my notebook?" I fumed. I was combing my fingers through my hair, which was a big tangled wad from a night in the tent. My eyes

The thief

were still foggy from sleep.

"I got up early," said Annie, all innocent. "I was reading through your clues to the kidnapping."

"What else are you reading?" I demanded.

"That's all," she said. "And a few of your letters to Katie. Is she your best friend?"

That did it.

"Yes, she's my best friend," I spat. "And you're not. So you have no business sticking your nose in my notebook!"

"I'm sorry," Annie said. "I didn't know—"

"Yes, you did know," I shot back. "You knew perfectly well my notebook is private. You're a snoop!"

Annie shut the notebook and threw it down. I didn't see it coming and it smacked me on the head.

"Thanks a lot!" I screamed at her.

"I didn't mean for it to hit your head," she apologized.

I wasn't in the mood to accept her apology. "Oh, sure!" I muttered. I snatched up my notebook and stormed back to the tent.

I started tearing the tent down all by myself.

"I'll help!" Annie called.

"Just stay put in your stupid tree!" I yelled. "I'd rather do it myself!"

I rolled up the sleeping bags and wrapped the stakes and poles into the tent. I was stomping around, furious. I tied it all up really hard because I was so mad. My dad wouldn't have believed I did it all alone—usually, I hate putting the camping gear away. But I was too angry to think about that now.

I stalked over to the fire. I sat down, still fuming, with my back to Annie. I started reading through the pages of my notebook, thinking of how she had read them without permission. Now she knew her stories had scared the wits out of me. Now she knew *all* about the angels, not just a little. Now she knew things I'd never intended her to know.

"I'm truly sorry, Hannah," she called from the tree.

I ignored her. *Sure!* I thought. *Sure she's really sorry!*

The fire was dwindling and starting to get really smoky. I took a stick and pushed the wood around to get it going again. The smoke poured out like huge clouds of fog.

The breeze blew the smoke right in my face. I started choking. As I backed off, something seemed to appear in the smoke. I squinted and stared hard. Yes! There *was* something there, in the thick white cloud of smoke!

Our campfire

Chapter 13

An Angel in the Smoke

I could make out a figure, which looked as if it were floating. And I heard faint music. It sounded like a beautiful voice, singing.

> *"Oh, blow, ye winds, over the ocean,*
> *And blow, ye winds, over the sea."*

It was Lyra. I knew it!

"Is that you singing, Hannah?" Annie called. So Annie could hear her, too!

"No, it's not me!" I said.

"Then who is it?" she asked.

I didn't want to tell her yet. She'd figure it out in a minute.

"My mom sings that song to me sometimes," Annie said, still in the tree. I think she was afraid I was still steaming and that I'd strangle her if she got too close.

But all of a sudden, I was finished being mad. Lyra had distracted me from it. I could see her huge wings unfolding. Sparks of brilliant white light spun around her and twinkled like teeny fireflies. She glided toward me, then back into the smoke as if she were dancing.

I listened hard to her words. They might be a message.

> *"Oh, blow, ye winds, over the ocean,*
> *And bring back my Bonnie to me."*

"Holy smokes, Hannah!" Annie cried. "That's one of your angels, isn't it?"

"Yes," I said, keeping my eyes on Lyra. "My music angel."

I waited for more singing, but I guess that was it. Lyra silently smiled, swirled herself up into the sky with the trails of smoke, and vanished.

"I've never heard anything so beautiful," said Annie. "That was awesome! Glory! I

Lyra

never would have believed it if I hadn't seen it with my own eyes!"

"It *is* amazing, isn't it?" I agreed. "But, more important, she was giving us a message and we have to figure it out."

"She was singing 'My Bonnie Lies over the Ocean,'" said Annie. "It's an old folk song."

I knew that song, too. We sang it in Ms. Crybaby's music class once or twice.

"Let's see," I murmured, trying to make a connection. "Windy ocean? Windy sea? Does it mean we have to cross a sea to bring Zack back?" I asked.

"I hope not," said Annie. "The Atlantic Ocean is awfully far from here."

"Is there any water around here where it gets windy?" I asked. "Maybe Zack is across the water someplace."

"Just the river," answered Annie. "It's right nearby."

"Does it get windy?" I asked.

"Oh, yeah! When there's a storm." Then Annie suddenly yelled, "Hannah, watch out!"

There was a crash, then a big thump! I turned around and saw that Annie wasn't in the tree anymore. She was lying in a heap at the bottom of the trunk, moaning.

What made her fall? Was Lyra back? I glanced at the fire. As I did, a huge cloud of smoke blew right at me, surrounding me like a mountain fog.

I ran through the smoke toward Annie. But then I smashed right into something. It felt like a person. I started screaming at the top of my lungs. In a split second, I realized Annie hadn't yelled out because of Lyra. She'd yelled—and fallen—because, through the smoke, she'd seen someone heading toward me. A man!

Chapter 14

Home in the Holler

I was terrified. There were no houses for miles around, so where could this guy have come from? Then I remembered how we'd felt we were being watched. Was it him? I quickly grabbed my walking stick for protection.

The man backed off and moved toward Annie. He looked a little like Santa—rosy cheeks and a long beard. And he had a belly that probably shook when he laughed. Except he wasn't dressed in red. He was wearing blue overalls.

"Let me help you there," he said to Annie, pulling her up. He actually said *thar* instead of *there*. "You don't want to go breakin' no bones now, Miss Jones."

He took a look at Annie's arms and legs. "Nothing broken. Just cuts and scrapes. We'll have to walk you to my place here in the holler and take care of those gashes," he said.

"Just hold on a minute!" I shouted. I raced over and stood right in front of him, my walking stick firmly planted.

"What's going on?" I asked. "Where are you taking her?" One kidnapping on this mission was enough.

"Now, don't go getting your dander up," he said. "My name is Jesse O'Brien." He extended his hand. I hesitated, but then accepted. Surprisingly, his handshake was warm and genuine.

Jesse O' Brien

"I've been livin' in these parts forever. I don't mean to cause any harm."

I watched his eyes while he talked. Sometimes you can tell if a person is trustworthy just by the look in their eyes. His eyes were sky blue and looked honest enough. But how could I know for sure?

"It's okay, Hannah," Annie said. "I've heard Zack talk about Mr. O'Brien now and then. You play a banjo, right?"

"That's right," he said. "Like flowin' honey. And Zack Jones comes visiting with his fiddle, his sweet cherrywood Valentine. We play on the porch sometimes at Joe's Store together."

"I thought so," said Annie. "Zack's my brother."

Jesse O'Brien smiled. "I guessed that. You and he have the same carrot-red hair."

"Okay, then," I said, as if I were making the decision here. "We'll go with you." But I still kept my guard up. I mean, how did we know this guy wasn't the kidnapper?

I tied our sleeping bags and tent onto our backpacks. Then I grabbed Annie's walking stick, just in case.

We got to his place, which was a cute little house in the holler. It was all lively, with flowers in front and a cat and a dog and a pig wandering

Jesse's House

around. Over on the side was a huge vegetable garden with a bunch of pumpkins. I saw an outhouse, too, fresh with paint—I guess that means he still uses it.

Inside, Mr. O'Brien offered Annie a seat on the couch. He brought her a bowl of water and a towel to clean the dirt from her cuts.

"You want sassafras tea or willow?" he asked.

"I'll take sassafras," said Annie, dabbing at her wounds.

"Me, too," I said. I had no idea what it was, but it sounded tastier than willow to me.

"I've also got pink lemonade made from mountain sumac," he added. I noticed he said it the mountain way: SHOE-mack. Annie and I exchanged a look.

"I'll stick with sassafras," I said. As I looked around, I saw a woodstove, herbs hanging from the rafters, and tins with labels on them. No sign of anyone kidnapped here. There was something in the oven that smelled really good.

"What are you baking?" I asked.

Mr. O'Brien winked at me. "It's my special secret recipe," he said. "A little sample of heaven for the festival."

He poured our tea. It smelled like root beer stick candy.

"Now, about those cuts," he said, opening a tin box. He pulled out a hunk of brown leaves and shoved them in his mouth.

"What's that?" I asked, still suspicious.

"Chewing tobacco," he replied. His mouth was all full and drippy. I gagged just looking at it.

Then I couldn't believe what I saw. Mr. O'Brien took the gob of soaking wet tobacco right out of his mouth and smushed it on

Tobacco dripping on Annie's cuts

Annie's cuts! Now I *really* gagged.

Annie shuddered, and looked at me all grossed out.

"This'll do the trick," said Jesse O'Brien. Then he taped bandages over the tobacco to hold it in place. I mean, the gross-out factor just kept getting worse!

"It'll start these gashes healing right away," Mr. O'Brien said.

It took everything in me not to barf right there on the floor.

"Some people say a spider's web works better," he continued. "But tobacco's always worked for me." He got up and went to the corner for his banjo.

"A spider's web?" I asked, totally confused.

"It's an old wives' tale," whispered Annie. "You lay the web right on the wound, and it's supposed to heal."

old wives' tale

I opened my mouth to say something rude. I guess Annie could tell because she quickly stopped me. "Shhh! Don't hurt his feelings!" she said. "I'll take this crud off as soon as we leave!"

Mr. O'Brien came back and sat down with his banjo. I think he'd made it himself from old car parts.

"So, what are you girls doing out in these parts?" he asked, strumming while he talked.

"Zack's been kidnapped," said Annie.

Mr. O'Brien frowned and made a twang with his thumb on the strings.

"Kidnapped?" he repeated. "Now, who would go and kidnap that boy?"

"We don't know for sure," said Annie. "But we think he's been taken to one of the houses in the strip mine ghost town."

Jesse stared at us, strumming and thinking. "You know," he said slowly, "I swore I saw smoke coming out of the old schoolhouse chimney last night."

"What?" yelled Annie. In a flash, she sprang to her feet, grabbed her pack, and headed for the door. She spun around. "You're talking about the old school by Dead Miner's Bridge, right?" she asked.

"That's the one," said Jesse, nodding.

"Then we're out of here!" Annie said, all excited. "Come on, Hannah! We've got no time to waste!"

Chapter 15

A Dang Scary Tale

"Whoa, there," said Jesse. "I'm just gettin' ready to leave for Joe Palmer's general store down the road. I'll drive you that far if you wait one sec."

"Okay," said Annie. "That'll save us some time."

"I'll just take my festival entry out of the oven and we'll head out," said Jesse, setting aside his banjo.

"There's a path behind the general store," Annie said to me. "We can hike from there to the schoolhouse."

I was kind of hoping we could drive *all the way* there. My feet were so tired from the walking we'd done, and I was also starting to get blisters. But I wasn't about to mention that to Jesse. I'm sure he'd have some gross cure for that, too!

Jesse's truck

The three of us hopped into Jesse's truck and headed north.

"So when did you find out about this kidnapping?" Jesse asked.

Annie looked at me. "Two nights ago," she said. "We got a very strange message."

I didn't say a word.

"Strange?" asked Jesse. "What kind of strange?"

"It was sewn into my quilt," Annie answered, cautiously. "And it glowed in the dark."

"Hmmm. Sounds to me like the handiwork of some Appalachian angel," said Jesse, not batting an eyelash.

"You believe in angels?" I asked.

"Sure," he replied, shifting gears so that we all jolted forward in the truck. "I can sense them now and again, especially when I'm out fishing in the shimmerin' sunshine."

"No!" I said.

"Oh, yeah, as sure as you're born," he said. "They smell like spring-bloomin' hyacinths, even in the middle of winter."

"Really?" I said amazed.

"It's like you're feeling all at peace with yourself, and you know everything is the way it should be," he added.

I didn't say any more. I didn't know if he was serious or just pulling my leg. I suppose that's how some people feel when I talk about *my* angels.

"So who's this here kidnapper?" he asked.

"We think it's Ben Turner," said Annie. "He might be trying to keep Zack out of the fiddling contest tonight."

"Dang! Well, of all the rotten, underhanded things to do! So Ben's probably got him locked up in the old schoolhouse, huh?" said Jesse.

"Maybe," said Annie. "But you know Zack— he's probably scaring the pants off Ben with that story about the dead miner's wife."

Jesse chuckled. The truck hit a bump. I could just feel what was coming next.

"Do you know that story, Hannah?" he asked.

"Nope," I said. *Great, here it comes*, I thought. *Another ghost story*.

"Well, it's a dang scary tale. It goes something like this," said Jesse. "There's a haint about the old schoolmarm…"

"Hannah doesn't know mountain words," Annie cut him off. "You have to tell it so she understands."

"Well, then, *you* tell it," said Jesse.

So Annie, in her poetic storytelling way, told me the story. "One stormy spring night, a cranky, skinny old schoolteacher got raging mad at her husband, who was a coal miner, because they had no money for groceries. She thought her husband had gambled

The schoolmarm   The miner

the money away. She chased him out of the schoolhouse, where he'd come to see her, throwing rocks at him. Then she chased him to the covered bridge."

"That poor man!" I said.

"The miner jumped into the river and tried to swim to safety. The floodwaters swelled up, and he drowned. The next morning, the teacher discovered that her husband had spent the money to buy a piece of farmland to surprise her. She dropped stone dead, right in the schoolhouse."

I was thinking about how Ms. Crybaby seemed wonderful and sweet compared to this horrible teacher.

"Now, she's haunted the school ever since. And when you cross Dead Miner's Bridge, she throws rocks at you, and you're likely to fall into the river below and drown, just like her poor miner husband."

"You're some storyteller," said Jesse. "I thought Joe at the general store was good. But you spin quite a yarn!"

"But I didn't finish," said Annie.

"Well, go ahead," said Jesse. "We're all ears."

"Sometimes," Annie continued, "the old schoolteacher paces back and forth in the attic of the schoolhouse. Some people have even heard her sobbing from the window as she looks out, waiting for her husband to return."

we're all ears!

"Is that the schoolhouse we're going to?"

"The very same," said Jesse.

"And is that the bridge we have to cross to get there?" I asked.

"Dead Miner's Bridge," said Jesse.

At that moment, we pulled up to the general store and got out.

Chapter 16

The General Store

There were baskets and wreaths and huge bouquets of dried flowers hanging from the rafters of Joe's porch. Joe was out there with his dog, hanging a sign:

PUT THE GREEN BACK IN SUMMERSTONE CREEK

Elvis

"Hey, Joe! Hey, Elvis!" said Jesse.

Elvis came over to lick my hand. He was a great big hound with saggy cheeks.

"How's our revegetation fund coming along there?" Jesse asked.

Our what *fund?* I wondered.

Joe pointed to a fishbowl filled with money. "We're at $715.26 today. After the festival, we ought to triple that."

"What's the money for?" I asked.

"Replanting that barren mess," said Jesse, shaking his head. "It's a crying shame up there by the strip mine. And down by the stream, the rocks are orange and the grass is brown."

Joe stepped down from the ladder and straightened out his sweater. He stood back and admired his sign. "We got the mining company to match whatever money we can raise by the end of the month," he said.

"So if you collect a thousand dollars, the mining company donates a thousand dollars, too?" asked Annie.

"That's the plan," said Joe. "Then we use that money to plant trees, grass, and wildflowers."

"Tryin' our darndest to make it look like Mother Earth again," added Jesse.

"So *that's* why you're in the pie-baking contest this year, isn't it?" asked Annie.

"Yessirree! If I win, it's two hundred dollars toward our green fund!" said Jesse proudly. "And I can't think of a better way to spend the winnings!"

Green fund

I suddenly remembered my angel money. I had twenty-five dollars in my backpack, and I didn't need to buy anything at Joe's Store. So I dug out the cash and tossed it in the fishbowl.

"The mountains thank you," said Joe, smiling.

"Now, down to business," Jesse said. "These two girls are headed out to the old schoolhouse to unkidnap Zack Jones."

"A kidnapping?" Joe's eyebrows shot up.

Jesse raised the palm of his hand. "It's a long story, Joe. I'll tell you in due time. But right now, I'm a trifle concerned about those rain clouds."

We all looked up to the sky. It was gray, dark and threatening.

"My truck ain't worth a hill of beans on that path to the bridge," said Jesse. "It's all overgrown."

Joe

Joe's baskets

"I think you two better stay here and wait it out," Joe said as he arranged a display of grapevine baskets.

"We can't wait," Annie said flatly. "My brother's in trouble."

"And the fiddling contest is tonight," I piped up. There was no way Annie and I could wait around the store knowing that Zack was being held hostage. We started wriggling into our yellow rain gear.

"Only fools would go out when a storm like this is rolling in," said Jesse, shaking his head.

"Well, then, call us fools," said Annie. "'Cause we're going!" She turned on her heel and started down the steps.

"Womenfolk. Never could figure 'em out," Jesse moaned.

Joe chuckled. "If I didn't have to tend the store, I'd go with you," he said. "You girls shouldn't go alone."

"We aren't alone," I said boldly. "The angels will protect us! The ones that smell like hyacinths, remember?"

Jesse nodded.

"Well, angels or no angels," said Joe, "I'm sending old Elvis with you."

He petted his big old friendly hound. "You got something of Zack's for him to smell?"

"Why?" I asked.

"He'll pick up Zack's scent and lead you right to him."

Annie rolled up the sleeve of my rain jacket.

"This shirt I lent you is actually Zack's," she said. She stuck the cuff under Elvis's nose and he sniffed it. It looked like Elvis knew exactly what to do.

"You behave now, Elvis," said Joe. "And if there's any trouble, you come back here for help." I swear, it seemed Elvis understood every word Joe said.

We hurried down the footpath around the back of the general store. A few raindrops began to fall. We knew we had to beat the storm, so

Taking off in the rain

↑
ELVIS

we started running. Elvis bolted way ahead of us. Our backpacks flopped up and down, and our slickers made a fast swish-swishy sound.

The rain started to come down really hard, and suddenly the whole sky lit up with lightning. The thunder that followed was so loud that it hurt my eardrums.

Elvis came galloping back, scared by the crashing sounds. He was soaked and looked miserable—exactly like I felt.

"Maybe Jesse and Joe were right," I said. "Maybe we ought to go back and wait out the storm." Another crack of thunder drowned out my words.

"What?" shouted Annie.

"Should we turn back?" I hollered.

"No way," yelled Annie. "We're not far from the bridge now."

Elvis and Annie dashed ahead through the driving rain. The stones and autumn leaves were slick under my feet. My shoes were packed with thick mud. I wasn't used to these paths, and I felt all clumsy, dragging behind.

"Hurry, Hannah! Hurry!" Annie yelled from up ahead. All I could see was pouring rain and tall trees. I had no idea how far there was to go. Elvis barked a few times, as if he was telling me to speed it up.

I struggled along, keeping my feet wide apart. I took giant, flat steps so I wouldn't slip and fall. I was remembering how I fell into a muddy grave in Australia once. It was covered with leaves, and I just toppled right in. I had to pull myself out with a rope! But I quickly stopped thinking about that—I had to keep my mind focused on my feet. Left foot, right foot, left foot, right…

"Hannah, keep going! You're almost here!" I heard Annie yell.

Up ahead, through the cold, stinging raindrops, I could see the bridge. It had a wooden roof that would cover us from the storm. I knew there wasn't much longer to go, so I ran as fast as I could. I really wanted to get out from under the rain. The bridge looked sort of like a long barn or tunnel. It was all dark inside. The wood was old and rickety. A few boards in the sides and the floor had broken off. Rusty nails were sticking out.

"We made it!" shouted Annie. "Dead Miner's Bridge!"

Elvis was running around in circles, anxious to keep going.

I squinted down the long, dark tunnel. All I could see was pitch black. Then I heard something terrible.

Chapter 17

Dead Miner's Bridge

Some sounds are really, really scary. In fact, I keep a page in my journal just for creepy sounds. Here are a few:

* Tree branches tapping on your window in the dark.
* Car tires crunching along in the middle of the night and stopping front of your house.
* A door creaking open for no reason.

And now, standing at one end of Dead Miner's Bridge, I heard sounds that will be ranked right up there on that list.

Crashing.

Smashing.

Massive waves of water hurling against the bridge.

There was one crash after another. The river rose up and slammed through the holes in the floorboards, shaking the bridge walls. It washed over the inside floors. We were drenched in a bashing flood of freezing cold water.

Annie looked petrified. She was twirling her hair hard around her fingers.

"I can see why people make up scary stories about this bridge," I said.

Dead Miner's bridge

"They're not made-up stories, Hannah," said Annie, her voice trembling. "The miner really did die in these waves."

I could see that Annie was scaring herself silly. The dark, the storm, and the wild river were bad enough. Now she was making it even worse with those folk tales.

"Maybe it is true, but that doesn't mean the miner is making these waves crash up now."

"How do you know?" shouted Annie. "See? Even Elvis is terrified."

I looked down at poor Elvis. He let out a whimper and backed up against the wall of the bridge, shaking.

"He's scared of the thunder, not the stories," I pointed out. "The miner and his wife do not haunt this place. I swear."

"You can't be sure of that," said Annie.

I took a deep breath. "I'll go across the bridge first. You and Elvis follow behind."

Annie looked like she had no intention of following me. But we had come this far and there was no way I was going to let any of us chicken out now, especially because of some superstitious story. My bossy side came out.

"Come on," I said pulling out my flashlight. "There'll be rain and thunder and crashing water on this bridge. But no miner. And no schoolteacher. I promise. Now, hurry up and follow me!"

I took a step into the dark. Then another. I walked carefully from board to board. I could hear the water rushing fast right below me. I stayed along the edge of the bridge, where the boards were sturdier. So far, so good. I beamed my flashlight back toward Annie. She and Elvis were still standing where I'd left them, cowering against the bridge entrance.

"I can't do it!" Annie moaned. It sounded like she was crying.

Just then, another huge wave hit. It crashed up from the river, flooded through the wood slats, and slapped me right in my face. Although it kind of stung, I stood still until the water had cleared. Then I flashed my beam in front of me.

There was a big gaping hole right at my feet! Three of the floorboards weren't there! One more step, and I would have fallen right into the raging river!

I almost fell in this hole.

I took a flying leap over the missing boards. But when my feet landed, another burst of water slammed against the bridge and crashed beneath me. I slipped right on my rear end.

I grabbed onto a heavy wood beam on the side of the bridge and clung on tight. With one hand, I reached around to my backpack. I fished out my rope. I tied one end on the beam and twisted the other end around my waist. That would hold me enough to keep me from falling in the river.

I glanced down through the slots in the floor. A beam of light was tossing around in the waves.

"Oh, no!" I yelled to Annie. "There goes my flashlight!" Not only was I shivering, wet, and frightened, but now I had no light and could barely see. I began to feel as if the end was near.

But just then, I felt a familiar tug on my hair. My head got yanked back, so luckily, my face just missed getting hit by another slapping wave.

"Hello, Hannah," said Demi's voice. "What seems to be the problem?"

"Problem? What's the problem?" I yelled back, clutching on to the wood beam for dear life. "Well, for starters, Zack is kidnapped, this bridge is going to collapse and drop me in the river any second, Annie's crying, Elvis is howling…"

You should have heard me babbling at the top of my lungs. I guess I was really scared.

"Calm down," said Demi quietly. "I'm here. There's nothing to be worried about."

But I couldn't calm down.

"I'm soaked to the bone and shivering," I whined. "And now you show up acting like everything's fine! I'm about to fall into this river and be swept away forever—I'd say there's plenty to be worried about!"

"Hannah," said Demi calmly, "why do you think I'm here? I know you're in trouble."

"So get me out of here!" I moaned. "Take me off this mission!"

"Your mission's almost finished," she said "And there really *is* light at the end of this tunnel."

Annie's flashlight shone into the bridge. "Where are you, Hannah?" she yelled.

"You need Annie, and Annie needs you," Demi said kindly. The sound of her voice was so tranquil that it began to comfort me.

"So what should I do?"

"You must allow Annie to help you across the bridge," said Demi. "She's braver than she knows. She'll discover it's not haunted, I promise."

"But she won't come!" I whined.

"What do you have that could coax her across?" asked Demi. Instantly, I thought of the rope. I untwisted it from my waist and tossed it into the dark tunnel toward Annie.

"Annie!" I hollered. "Grab the end of the rope! It's tied to the bridge!"

"Good work!" said Demi. There was Annie's flashlight, making its way toward me, slow but sure.

"I'll be with you every step of the way," said Demi.

"Promise?" I asked.

"I promise," Demi answered.

At that very moment, Annie jumped across the gaping hole in the floor and landed next to me, rope in hand. Elvis leaped beside her.

"Are you okay, Hannah?" she asked, helping me to my feet.

"Yeah, I'm fine," I said. "But I think you should lead the way. I'm not doing too great a job."

"Okay," said Annie.

She seemed to have mustered up her courage. Maybe because she thought I was in trouble. Well, she was right—I *was* in trouble.

We headed on toward the end of the bridge. The rain and waves seemed to be quieting down.

Then suddenly, we heard clattering on the roof. It sounded like rocks were being hurled at us from every direction.

Elvis let out a horrific howl.

Annie grabbed a hold of me, terrified.

"It's just like in the story," she gasped. "The schoolmarm's rocks!"

Chapter 18

Schoolhouse Lessons

Annie's grip on me tightened as the clatter got louder. It was deafening. Suddenly, it occurred to me what it was.

"Hail!" I hollered, over the racket. "It *sounds* like rocks, Annie, but it's really just hail!"

The hail was coming down as marble-sized ice balls, right through the roof and side walls of the bridge. My hands and face stung where they hit me.

Annie covered her head and gave me a big smile.

"You're right!" she hollered back. "Pull your hood up, Hannah."

We inched on ahead through the bridge. Before we knew it, there really *was* a light at the end of the tunnel, just like Demi had said.

"We made it!" yelled Annie, above the clatter

of the hail. "No dead miner grabbed us! No dead schoolmarm, either!"

"See, this bridge *isn't* haunted!" I said.

"I know," said Annie, triumphantly. "It's just a story. A really great scary story, but just a story..."

We peered through the storm toward the old school.

"Look ahead!" Annie yelled. "There's a light in the schoolhouse!"

the old school house

"I see it!" I yelled back. It was the only spot of light on the whole rainy mountainside. We could make out someone's shadow moving across one of the lower windows. Ben's dirt bike was lying by the front steps.

We crouched low and crept toward the school. Now that the hail was dwindling, we could hear music.

"'The Devil Went Down to Georgia,'" shouted Annie.

The wild music was blaring louder, even through the rain. "What a perfect song for a kidnapper!" I hollered.

Suddenly, Elvis sniffed the air. He let loose with a wild howl and went barreling toward the school. He attacked the front door, scratching and whining.

"Oh, no!" yelled Annie. "Elvis picked up Zack's scent! He's going to give us away!"

We tore off after him. Annie grabbed him by the collar, and we dashed around the side of the school. Just then, the music stopped. Ben had turned off his tape player. We heard the front door creak open.

"Who's there?" hollered Ben into the rainy night.

Of course, we didn't answer. But we did look at each other, giggling silently.

"I have a great idea!" Annie whispered in my ear. "Let's scare the pants off Baloney Breath!"

"How?" I asked.

"Grab some stones and follow me."

We loaded our pockets with muddy stones. Then Annie and I scrambled up the fire escape on the side of the school. When we hoisted ourselves up, the metal bars wobbled and made a monstrous creaking sound. Elvis waited for us below.

We peeked in the tiny window by the fire escape. Zack was stuck inside a broom closet. He was sitting on the floor with Valentine, looking really lonely.

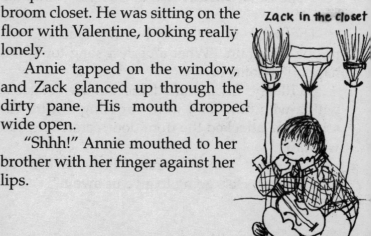

Zack in the closet

Annie tapped on the window, and Zack glanced up through the dirty pane. His mouth dropped wide open.

"Shhh!" Annie mouthed to her brother with her finger against her lips.

Perfect!

We scurried on up the fire escape like rats in the rain. There was a big window at the top that we climbed in.

The attic was dark and dreary. I wiped the cobwebs from my face and shook off the rain. Down below, we heard Ben ranting away.

"If you're lucky, I'll let you out of there in a few hours!" he roared, all bossy. "By then, I'll have the two hundred dollars all to myself."

Fire escape

"I feel sorry for your greedy soul, Ben Turner!" Zack called back from inside the closet. "You're a decent fiddler, but you've got a heck of a bad attitude!"

Baloney Breath snickered. "I'm gonna get me a brand-new dirt bike," he bragged. "What would *you* spend the money on? That stupid green fund?"

"You're gonna pay for what you've done," said Zack. "Who was at the front door, anyway? The dead miner?"

"Shut yer yap, Jones!" yelled Ben. "Nobody was there!"

That's when Annie got her plan in gear. She shuffled across the floor of the attic and took big, slow steps that made the floorboards creak.

"Somebody's up there!" shouted Ben, nervously.

"Oh, it's probably just the dead schoolteacher pacing the floor," said Zack calmly.

"Stop it!" yelled Ben. He sounded scared. "Just shut up!"

"You know the story," Zack continued. "How the old teacher threw rocks at her husband until he jumped in the floodwater..."

At that moment, right on cue, Annie and I took the stones from our pockets and hurled them at the floor.

"What the heck?" yelled Ben. We could hear him scrambling around down below like a scared rabbit.

"And on certain nights...," Zack continued.

"Dang!" yelled Ben. "I told you to shut yer trap!"

"...you can hear the teacher screaming out the window..."

Annie let out a shrill wail. Elvis scratched the floor, whining and howling. I had to cover my mouth with both hands to keep my laughter quiet.

"I'm outta here!" hollered Ben. We heard his boots scramble across the room as he bolted out the front door. He grabbed his bike, revved it up, and disappeared across the bridge.

Chapter 19

The Festival

"You can come out now!" Zack called.

Annie and I flew down the stairs down to free him. We were laughing so hard, we couldn't even talk. We slid back the wood latch and unlocked the closet door.

"That was the best trick ever!" Zack said. "Baloney Breath is scared to death!"

"Scared enough to never try kidnapping some-body again!" said Annie, all proud of our work.

"How did you guys find me?" asked Zack.

"It's a long story," I said.

"A long, true story," said Annie. "And you know how truth can be stranger than fiction!"

"But we'd better hustle if you're going to make it to the festival!" I said.

We dashed out the door, with Annie leading the way. Elvis met us outside. He jumped all over

Zack and licked his face. "What's *he* doing here?" Zack asked.

"That's part of the long story," I said.

The storm had let up, but we could still hear the crashing thunder far in the distance. We rushed back across the bridge, jumping carefully across the missing floorboards. Zack almost fell right through, too, but Annie and I grabbed him just in time! We made it to Joe's Store within twenty minutes.

"Well, lookee here!" said Jesse, all bright-eyed. "Zack's back and fit as a fiddle!"

"We were worried about you, Zack!" said Joe. "Are you gonna make it on time for the contest?" Now he was filling jars with licorice sticks—red and black and brown.

Licorice sticks

red black brown

"You've barely got half an hour," said Jesse.

"He's just *got* to get back in time," pleaded Anne. "We've come so far already."

Jesse picked up his keys. "Come on, I'll drive you over to the festival! My truck's right outside."

We all piled in, including Elvis. The truck rumbled up and down the muddy hills until we came to a big park full of people and trees and music. There was a soaking wet banner strung across the entrance. It was the one the signmakers had made at Annie's house.

SUMMERSTONE CREEK
FALL FESTIVAL
FRIDAY, SATURDAY, SUNDAY

Music was coming from everywhere. Even though there had been a big rain, no one's spirits seemed dampened. Everywhere you looked, people were smiling.

The festival was full of good stuff.

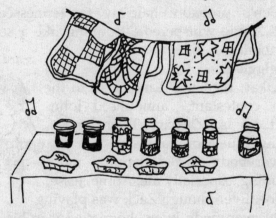

"There they are!" yelled Annie's mom. She waved us through the crowd and over to the music stage. "Where have you three been? We've been worried sick about you!"

"These young folk have had themselves one humdinger of an adventure!" said Jesse.

"I'll tell you about it later, Mom!" called Zack as he and Valentine headed for the stage.

"You certainly will," I heard his mom say in a low voice. I guess she was more glad to see him than angry with him.

"Next fiddler up is—Benjamin Seth Turner!" called the announcer (who just happened to be Annie's dad).

No response.

"Ben Turner?" he hollered again.

We all looked around. There wasn't a trace of old Baloney Breath.

"Ben's probably halfway to Tennessee by now," Annie whispered. "Running like a scared jackrabbit!"

I giggled.

Zack on stage

"Okay, then, we'll move on to the next contestant," announced John. "Next up is…Zachary Tyler Jones, playing 'Blue Mountain Girl'!"

Everybody started clapping and whooping, especially me, Annie, Jesse, and Joe. Even though Zack was playing a song everybody knew, he played it in his own special way. It was a very sweet tune, about a very special girl. By the time he finished, Annie

Dancing to Zack's fiddle

and I were all teary-eyed. Just about the whole crowd was screaming for more.

When Zack took his bow, a bunch of admirers crowded around him. Out of the corner of my eye, I saw the judges smile. He had that two hundred dollars all wrapped up.

I couldn't believe what I saw next.

"Annie, look who's coming through the crowd!" I whispered.

Ben Turner! He stepped onto the stage. I saw Jesse roll up his sleeves, ready for a fight.

"Zack Jones," said Ben, staring Zack right in the eyes. "I have just one thing to say to you—right here in front of all these people…"

Zack's eyes opened wide. He took a step forward, ready for a confrontation.

"You're the absolute, honest-to-gosh, best dang fiddle player in all these mountains," Ben said. "And I am truly sorry for trying to keep you from playing tonight."

Ben dug into his pocket as he stared down at the ground. "Here's your lucky bandanna," he said. "I hope you can forgive me."

Zack was speechless. He took his purple bandanna from Ben and tied it around his leg. Ben reached out his hand, and Zack shook it. Then a big grin broke across Zack's face.

"Go grab your fiddle, Ben Turner!" he hollered. "Let's show these folks what good bluegrass music sounds like!" A few other fiddlers jumped on stage and played "The Devil Went Down to Georgia."

The crowd went wild as the music started up

again. We linked arms and danced around while Zack played his tune. Then Annie pulled me aside.

"I've got something to tell you," she whispered.

"I've got something to tell you, too," I said.

"You first," said Annie.

"Well," I said, "I'm going to be heading back any minute. My trip is done, and my angels will be sending me home."

"Already?" said Annie. She looked really disappointed. "Well, promise not to be a stranger, okay? I have an idea—let's be pen pals! You can send me notes from Wisconsin."

"And you can send me notes from Blue Mountain," I said, smiling. "Let's do it!"

I pulled out my journal, and we wrote down each other's addresses.

"Well, before you go," said Annie, "I want to thank you for encouraging me."

"I encouraged you?" I said, astonished. "How?"

"I'm sorry I read your journal," she said. "But that's where I found out that my stories really scared you. It helped me see that I'm pretty good at telling tales. So I've entered the storytelling competition!"

"Dang!" I said, talking like Jesse.

"I've decided to tell an original tale, one that I made up myself. If it's really good, maybe someday the folks who hear it will pass it on to their kids."

"What's it called?" I asked.

"'The Angels and the Kidnapped Fiddler,'" said Annie, all proud. "It may sound like just a tale, but I swear every word is true."

Both Annie and I laughed. "Dang!" I said again. I had to write this down for Katie. I sat under a big maple and began scribbling.

Friday night

Dear Katie,

Whew! The storm cleared up and...

That was it, the last of my notes to Katie from Blue Mountain.

Chapter 20

Quilting a Story

"Hannah, look what you're sitting on!" whispered Katie.

I was back, and underneath me, spread out perfectly, was a handmade quilt.

"You went...and came back...while I..." Katie's eyes were popping out of her head. "Where did you go?" she whispered.

"The Appalachian Mountains," I said. I felt like I was still there. In my head, I could hear Zack's fiddle playing "Blue Mountain Girl." And Annie's voice telling the story of the old schoolhouse kidnapping.

"You filled a bunch of pages in your science notebook!" Katie said as she grabbed it to read.

My Appalachian Angel Qv

I was back, all right. Katie was reading all about my trip, my cattail was still all soft and fuzzy on top, Jimmy Fudge's face was as red as the sumac now. Yep, things seemed to be back to normal.

"Go get the first-aid kit from the bus," Ms. Crybaby told Fudge dryly. "You'll be treating your rash yourself."

I wanted to jump up and put soggy, chewed-up tobacco leaves on his face and then bandage it up all tight, just like Jesse would have done.

"There's calamine lotion in the kit," said Ms. Crybaby. "It's pink. Just dab it all over your face."

I pictured Fudge coming back, looking like a frosty mug of pink lemonade. Just what he deserved! He trotted off, head-down, to the bus. Now all the attention he was getting was everyone laughing at him.

But, one by one, everybody started looking at my quilt.

"Hannah!" said Ms. Crybaby. "I didn't notice your quilt before!" She ran her fingers along the edge. "It's handmade!"

"Yes," I said. "Some friends of mine made it themselves." (I was talking about my angels, of course!)

I looked at the designs on the squares. I couldn't believe it. There was a square of Dead Miner's Bridge. And one of Joe's general store. There were a fiddle, a banjo, and a guitar. Jesse's pig. Elvis. The outhouse. And on each corner was a hand-sewn angel. They were all there: Aurora, Demi, Lyra, and Lorielle. It was a journal of my mission stitched on a quilt!

"Your friends are very talented," said Ms. Crybaby. "The only place I've seen work so beautiful is in the Appalachian Mountains!"

Katie stifled a giggle.

"Perhaps your friends can visit the class someday," she added.

"That would be nice," I said. I couldn't exactly tell Ms. Crybaby that my friends visit class all the time. And that everything on the quilt told a true story—the story of what happened while I was supposedly sitting right here on this field trip.

"Hey, here comes a raccoon!" yelled Kevin McPherson. We all turned to look. A little critter waddled out of the bushes and circled my quilt. Of course, I checked out her paw right away.

"Oh my gosh!" hollered Katie. "She's got a heart-shaped mark right on her paw!"

"That's not all she's got!" shouted Kevin.

There, waddling in a little row behind her, were three baby raccoons. They circled the quilt and followed their mom right back into the woods.

Mama and her babies

As I watched them go, I thought about what Annie said, and I smiled. She was absolutely right. Truth *is* stranger than fiction.

Bye now! See you on my next mission!

COOL APPALACHIAN STUFF

Appalachian Mountains—These are the oldest mountains in North America, millions of years older than the Rockies. They go all the way from northern Alabama up to Quebec, Canada. West Virginia is the only state located completely in Appalachia.

Apple butter—Kind of like thick applesauce. The apples get cooked and stirred until they're creamy. You eat the apple butter on biscuits or bread.

Artesian well—Water bubbling up from the ground. It's under pressure from the rocks below, so it rises to the surface, making a pool. When I was in Australia, I didn't see the biggest one on earth, which is the Great Australian Artesian Basin. It covers almost 700,000 square miles!

Bluegrass music—A special kind of country music played in a group. There's usually a fiddle, a banjo, a mandolin, and sometimes a guitar. It's very fast and fun to dance to. It started out in the southern Appalachian mountains, where there were a lot of Scottish and Irish settlers, but bluegrass didn't get its name until the 1950s.

Crafts—There are so many beautiful things people still make by hand in the Appalachian Mountains: quilts, baskets, wood carvings, rag dolls, wooden toys, musical instruments (like Jesse's banjo), log houses, metal tools, candles, and a whole bunch of other great stuff.

Fiddlers—These musicians keep the past alive by playing old folk songs that have been passed down for generations. They play songs of all kinds: for working, celebrating, or soothing babies to sleep.

Flapdoodle—Blackberries in a sweet sauce. I had it with hot biscuits and butter. Yummy!

Folk tales—Old stories that are told about life in the mountains: mining accidents, Civil War battles, strange deaths, and interesting people. These tales are passed down from one generation to the next, so it's hard to tell whether they're fact or fiction.

Good and bad mushrooms—Golden chanterelles are golden orange and delicious. Jack-o'-lanterns look almost exactly like them and are very poisonous. They are brighter orange, and their stems grow together at the base. (By the way, they don't have faces like Halloween pumpkins!) Like Annie says, never eat a mushroom unless you're absolutely, *positively* sure it's not poisonous.

Holler—Doesn't just mean "to yell"! It's also a name for "hollow," which is a narrow valley between the mountains—where most people in the West Virginian Appalachians live.

Home remedies—Lots of mountain people still use old-fashioned cures when they're hurt or sick. Some work great, and some don't work at all. (It depends on who you talk to.) Jesse uses chewed-up tobacco for cuts, dandelions to get rid of skin rashes, and catnip to make measles go away. Some people think if you cover a cut with a spider's web, it will heal.

Mining—Coal is needed for fuel, and there are two ways to mine it from the mountains. The old way was to make underground tunnels, dig the coal out with picks and shovels, and carry it out on coal cars. Now strip mining is more popular. The good thing is it's faster and cheaper to get at the layers of coal. The bad thing is that the tops get sliced right off the mountains. It's ugly, and it ruins the environment.

Quilting bee—When a bunch of friends get together to make a quilt, they call it a "bee." They talk and laugh, and get beautiful quilts made at the same time. Then they give the quilt for a wedding present or to raise money for things like Joe's green fund.

Raccoons—Furry gray critters who usually only come out at night. They wash their food before they eat it, and their paws are like human hands—they can peel all the corn in your garden, eat it, and leave the cobs behind while you're fast asleep. (I like their faces—they look like masked bandits.)

Ramps—Wild onions that grow in the spring. They smell so strong that if you eat them, your breath and your perspiration will smell like onions for days. Some schools in West Virginia have a rule that says you can't eat ramps and come to school or you'll be suspended. That's how bad they smell!

Sassafras—A kind of laurel tree. Its roots are used to flavor candy, soft drinks, and tea. I think it tastes a lot like root beer.

Sumac—Pronounced SHOE-mack in parts of the Appalachians, especially in West Virginia. You can make pink lemonade out of red sumac berries. Poison sumac has white-green berries, which hang like grapes when they grow. Poison sumac is a lot like poison ivy—if you touch it, you can get a skin rash, and even nasty blisters. (Believe me, I know!)

Willow—A tree with branches that are thin and flexible, so they're used to make baskets and wreathes. Weeping willow trees have leaves and branches that are droopy, so they look a little sad. Some people make tea from the bark of willow trees. I didn't try it, but Jesse says it's good for what ails you.

Here's a sneak peek at

Hannah and the Angels #5:
Saving Uncle Sean

Available wherever books are sold!

"We have to turn back!" the captain bellowed. "The storm's too fierce!"

The ferry lurched sideways, hurling Molly and me against the metal rail. We grabbed each other tight and planted our feet against the waves. The wind roared across the Atlantic. The rain stung our faces.

Just an hour ago, the clouds had looked all soft, like angel wings. But now they hung like a gloomy dark ceiling, drizzling cold, dropping hard rain on our heads. There were no more rainbows and no more sunbeams. Even in my thick sweater and heavy boots, I was freezing. I swear my bones were shivering.

Suddenly, I heard an eerie sound. It was a high-pitched cry, the exact sound of an E note on my flute. I listened hard.

Eeeeee! Eeeeee!

"Dolphins!" shouted Molly. She could hear it, too! "It's the dolphins from Dingle!" she cried.

"Impossible!" the captain hollered. "They never swim this far north!"

But I could see them, too. I saw fins diving through the wild waves right where Molly was pointing.

"See?" shouted Molly. "I told you!"

"Saints preserve us!" yelled the captain.

"They swam all the way from Dingle!" yelled Molly, jumping up and down. "Listen, Hannah! Can you hear? They came to bring us a message!"

Earn Your Golden Wings!

If you've acted like Hannah and helped someone else,
you are eligible to receive a special *Hannah and the
Angels* golden wings gift. Fill out the coupon below
with details of how you acted like an angel
(attach additional sheets if necessary).

To receive your FREE gift, mail to:

Random House Children's Publishing
Earn Your Wings Promotion
201 East 50th Street, MD 30-2
New York, NY 10022

- -

Name: _____ Age: ____

Address: _____

_____

I was an angel when I _____

_____

_____

_____

_____

Available while supplies last. Offer ends March 31, 1999. ***All coupons
must be received by Random House before 5:00 p.m. EST on that date.***
Limit: One per customer. Not valid with other offers. Multiple requests,
mechanical reproductions, and facsimiles will not be honored.
Reproduction, sale, or purchase of this coupon is prohibited. Random
House reserves the right to reject any forms not deemed genuine.
Valid only in the United States. Please allow 6-8 weeks for delivery.